Breakfast with the
Island Mystic

Breakfast with the Island Mystic

Parables for a New Christianity

Dr. F. W. (Mike) Luedde

iUniverse, Inc.
New York Lincoln Shanghai

Breakfast with the Island Mystic
Parables for a New Christianity

iUniverse books may be ordered through booksellers or by contacting:

iUniverse
2021 Pine Lake Road, Suite 100
Lincoln, NE 68512
www.iuniverse.com
1-800-Authors (1-800-288-4677)

This is a work of fiction. All of the characters, names, incidents, organizations and dialogue in this novel are either the products of the author's imagination or are used fictitiously.

ISBN-13: 978-0-595-40028-7 (pbk)
ISBN-13: 978-0-595-84413-5 (ebk)
ISBN-10: 0-595-40028-0 (pbk)
ISBN-10: 0-595-84413-8 (ebk)

Printed in the United States of America

CONTENTS

"Be careful: today's metaphors are tomorrow's idols."

—The Island Mystic

INTRODUCTION

THE WORD IN THE WORDS

Are you searching for God's Word? Try looking under a rock, or in the eyes of your lover, or in the eyes you see in a mirror. Try the wonder of a pelican in flight, or a moment of peace, or a Bach fugue. If you're still looking, open a book and read a story. In fact, read the stories in this book. God's Word is in them. Of course, God's Word is in all that is. All you need are eyes that can see it, ears that can hear it, and a heart that can intuit it. Those are essential equipment for the spiritual life.

The stories in this book are about life, and God, and Jesus, and you. And the Word of God is in every one of them.

None of that should surprise you. After all, stories create our lives. We don't invent stories, edit them, tell them, write them, change them, and publish them. What really happens is that stories invent us. They are part of the way that God creates us. Our lives are like shapeless clay until stories give them shape. Our view of life is an undifferentiated mass of disconnected perceptions until stories give them meaning.

Potters say that their work allows them to find the pot that is hidden in a ball of clay. She sits at the wheel hoping to discover how Spirit will flow from her fingertips to birth a vessel. Sometimes a pot emerges only to collapse. Sometimes a pot flies apart as the wheel spins. And sometimes a beautiful vessel rises as the potter lifts and caresses the clay. Then the potter looks with amazement at what formed, as though on its own, as the wheel spun. In creative pottery the vessel is the result of a subtle dialog between potter and clay. The potter's skill makes manifest what was hidden.

Telling and reading stories is like making pots. The teller of stories does not create something out of nothing. Rather, the storyteller listens to the voices of life, gives them expression, and then shares them with the reader. A *good* story reflects the life of the one who wrote it. A *very good* story reflects the lives of those who read it. And a *true story* reflects the Word of God. Think of the Word as that hidden pot in the ball of clay, patiently waiting in all that is and ever shall be for the storyteller to gather words into patterns like particles of clay. Finally, a *really, really true story* may become myth. Myths bring to life what the reader or listener already knows but didn't know that she knows. When a story expresses the reader's reality—the hungers of the heart, the yearning and desire for fullness to replace emptiness, the deep need to make sense out of what seems absurd—and gives it meaning, then the story carries the Word of God. It does this even when it is not a religious story. In fact, it may do this precisely because it is *not* religious, for religion is too often not about life but about escape from it into crusty concepts derived from someone else's experience, while God's Word is found more often in everyday experience than in temples. Holy stories are usually ordinary. They talk of mangers and stables, wars and executions, crosses and pilgrimages, and healings and confrontations. Holy stories are like lights that shine in our imaginations to show us the way life really is and what it could become.

"In the beginning was the Word." We know that familiar line because someone, whom we know as John, told us stories about a wild man who dunked people in a river, a young sage who liked to hang out with fishermen, some righteous people who got so caught up in religion that they lost their grip on reality, a couple of corrupt kings, and an empty hole in the ground. We remember John's stories. They shape our lives, our culture, and our history.

But we rarely remember what professionally religious people derive from the stories. Academics try to jam the Word of God into books of theology. Ecclesiastical assemblies try to freeze-dry it and store it in doctrines.

But at Christmas or Easter, at Ramadan or at Hanukkah we don't recite works of theology. We don't light candles so that we can recite books of confessions or catechisms. After all, who can remember those words? Who really cares about them? Remember that every doctrine and every work of theology begins with an attempt to understand a story. It is not Aquinas' *Summa*, Augustine's *Confession*, Barth's *Church Dogmatics*, or Tillich's *Systematic Theology* that stirs our hearts to pray. Our hearts are stirred by stories that refresh the Word in our daily lives. Works of theology will pass, but tales like that of David's victory over Goliath will endure forever, because there is something of both David and Goliath within each of us.

When old theologies wear out it's time to tell old stories in new ways. I remember sitting beside my mother in the colonial-style Presbyterian church that my family attended. I didn't like going to worship. The liturgy was one of those "three hymns, a prayer, an offering, and a sermon" affairs that encouraged passivity in the congregation. I was bored, restless, and often angry. Deep inside, even when I was a small child, I wondered how a God of love's power could be worshipped with such impotence. My favorite part of the service was the benediction: the pastor's words were warm and loving, and when he finished we all got permission to leave. But even in that fortress of mediocrity I experienced a few inspiring moments. One of them happened when I stood in the balcony singing "I Love to Tell the Story." I wasn't sure what the story really was, but I was moved by the feeling of the people as they sang. I don't think that they knew the story either since no one told it outside of church. I always wondered how people could sing that they love to do something they rarely did. But that hymn had power because of the powerful story behind it.

Sadly, these days many of the most popular stories in Christianity are not about Jesus. They are not about living an abundant, passionate, overflowing life. They are not about falling in love with the Divine whose presence penetrates every moment. Mostly they are about death and spiritual elitism. The hottest selling "Christian" literature today is not about leading a more loving and contemplative life. It's about surviving the end of the world. Survival has always been the core issue in "apocalyptic" writing. People who live in fear want to know that they will survive. They want to be part of the religiously privileged that is raptured into outer space where they will be safe from trouble and suffering. That kind of writing appeals to the worst side of our personalities: we feel secure in God's grasp and gloat over the failure of others who are left behind. Too many stories about the end of time feed the same kind of Pharisaical self-righteousness that crucified Jesus.

Why this fascination with the end of things? We fear the end for lots of reasons. America has finally experienced vulnerability. Until 9/11 we were never attacked at home by an alien force. We've always had our share of homegrown terrorists, as we did at Oklahoma City and Columbine. We have our crazy serial killers lurking around abortion clinics and Luddites sending letter bombs to high-tech professors. We have our militias, our gangs, our Klan, our civil war, and our culture war. But it wasn't until thirteen foreign fanatics crashed airplanes into buildings that we got really scared. Apparently we tolerate kooks as long as they are our own.

These events, traumatic though they are, are not signs of the end. The world is not coming to an end, despite all the wars, earthquakes, global economic crises, environmental deterioration, and acts of terrorism. But we face a different kind of "end" that shakes our souls to their depths. We try to avoid this end by pretending that the apocalypse is near. It is the end of "isms." The old religions and philosophies that held our fears at bay don't work anymore. Our old spiritual support systems either petrify into rigid moralism or become completely dysfunctional. New ones have yet to be fully born. In this age of spiritual transition, there aren't many choices. We can trust in God's loving Presence, we can heroically stand alone in the universe without belief, or we can retreat into fundamentalism (which looks identical whether it takes the form of Christianism, Islamism, Hinduism, or nationalism).

Even fundamentalism is an "ism," and we are witnessing the death of all the old isms. Communism, a religion masquerading as a political and economic system, has few serious followers today. Disciples of Islamism show their spiritual bankruptcy by carrying suicide bombs and hijacking airplanes, even though true Muslims seek a deeper heart in the rediscovered teachings of the Sufis. Christian themes of love, peace, joy, freedom, and forgiveness have been replaced in the popular press by the legalism and spiritual bankruptcy of Christianism. Because of the vacuity of traditional western religions spiritual seekers now look to the east. They have made the Dalai Lama and the (Zen) monk Thich Nhat Hanh into best selling authors, even though those who buy their books usually don't embrace Buddhism in its traditional forms. We are at loose ends. The end is near.

There is a wonderful freedom in having all these loose ends flying around. If we have the eyes to see the hand of God at work, we will marvel at the creativity of the Spirit. God is no longer the property of the churches, but of the people. Spirituality is no longer circumscribed by religion, but is free for all to explore as the Spirit moves their hearts. Sacred events now happen in ordinary secular culture. Monasteries become retreat centers where all are welcome without regard to denominational loyalties. Twelve-step programs offer spiritual communities far more open and committed to honest confession than are most Christian congregations. Networks of seekers explore spiritual direction, healing, contact with other religions, and new forms of prayer. Secular publishers discover profit in feeding those who hunger for depth they don't find in Sunday Schools. House churches and small groups allow new spiritual intimacy. New forms of church emerge in networks of people who meet in cell groups or share on the Internet. It is the end of religious isms as we have known them. It is also the beginning.

And in all this change the Word of God endures forever. The scriptural stories still speak to our hearts: Moses talks with a bush in the wilderness, or Jesus breaks cultural rules to give love to a woman beside a well in enemy territory, or Paul discovers the blindness of his fanaticism on the Damascus road. The stories are everlasting. The religion we have built on them is not, nor is the collection of theology and doctrine we have derived from them.

And so, for the sake of Jesus, it is time to tell new stories about the old stories. Most of the new stories we tell will pass away, but every new story told with trust in God will help us better understand the old ones. And every new story told with prayer will contain, tucked somewhere in its words, the loving Word of God.

I met the Island Mystic on a foggy winter day. Most of his stories are about the old stories. I suspect he was around when they were written. I felt serene when I was with him even though much of what he taught upset me. When I weighed anchor and left his lagoon, I knew that his words were true for me. God's Word was hidden in them. I have thought deeply about them since that day. In the Epilog, I'll give you some of my thoughts about what he taught.

In the meantime, I share his words with you in the hope that you also will meet him when your life is foggy and you don't know what course to sail.

And remember, God will welcome you at the gate of heaven with an embrace, not a theology exam. Let your heart play and your mind relax!

CHAPTER 1

▼

THE EMERALD LAGOON

In the middle of my life I found myself lost in a fog of unknowing. When Dante was lost in the woods, Beatrice helped him find his true path. But Dante wasn't a sailor. Here on the Texas gulf coast you're more likely to be lost in fog than in forests. When that happened to me, a few dolphins showed me the rhumb line. Maybe one of them was Beatrice...?

I once thought I knew the course of my life. I thought I knew most of the answers. I knew how to find the ones I was missing. I was a spiritual director, a healer of souls and custodian of truth. But a time came when I no longer believed that being spiritual was about knowing answers. In fact, it seemed to have more to do with figuring out the right questions.

I was burned out.

It wasn't that I didn't believe in Jesus anymore. I trusted him more deeply than ever. But the old ways of being Christian held less and less meaning for me.

And it wasn't that I didn't love spiritual direction. I did. My directors have guided me through many dangerous storms. Spiritual direction is a sacred endeavor. The directee's insight and the director's advice are far less important than the loving Spirit that moves between them. But sometimes even that's not enough.

I discovered my lostness one foggy morning in late Fall. My heart was becalmed, empty of the Spirit's breezes. I had lost the will to listen as others talked about their lives' voyages while my own vessel was moored to her pier. I wanted to untie my life, sail away, and let the canvas carry me to new truths.

My sloop, *Moonghost*, was named after a missionary priest who surfed during the full moon while wearing a white cassock. The natives called him "the ghost who walks on water." I thought about Jesus when I named her. He went sailing with his friends when the crowds pressed against his soul. Sailing was a good escape for him. I always felt strangely close to him when I took the helm alone. While it's true that a boat is a hole in the water into which the owner throws money, I rationalized my boat payments by telling myself that I was doing what Jesus did when he needed some solitude. My boat was my hermitage.

My heart grew lighter every time I stepped aboard *Moonghost* and felt her move beneath me. She was a soulful mistress awaiting my touch, and I loved her dearly. Boarding a sailboat is like approaching the altar for communion. The hull and rigging create a sacred sanctuary floating on a sea of Spirit. On this foggy day we were a congregation of two as I stroked her gunwales, rigged her main halyard, coiled her jib's furling line, and started the cranky diesel auxiliary that pounded like a beating heart in her depths. I cast a hopeful glance at the masthead fly, looking for signs of a breeze, only to see the mast disappear into a hovering cloud. Mist wrapped nearby boats in a foggy shroud. I might get lost between my slip and the harbor entrance, but it wouldn't matter. I was lost anyway. I cast off and backed away from the pier.

I have always sought perfect solitude. I have longed to merge with nature's sacredness and experience God's beauty uncontaminated by civilization. Ghosting through fog on a sailboat creates an illusion of such solitude shared only by Spirit. If there were other boats in the channel, I couldn't see or hear them. I was alone.

God is uncharted mystery. Our religions give us the illusion that we know our way around the divine. But when we think we have mapped God, we quickly find that our charts don't represent reality. As I left the security of the channel for the expanse of the open bay, the familiar waterways I had sailed for years became a cloudy mystery. I recognized nothing. I saw no navigation aids. The silver cloud enveloped everything.

Mystery is wonderful but confusing. It calls us from mental apathy and sometimes scares us. I quickly realized that this voyage was foolish and dangerous as land disappeared into gray sameness off my stern. I laid my hand to the wheel to reverse course but something stopped me. My heart was under a relentless order to press on.

A mile or so farther east the foghorn on the sea-buoy comforted me like the voice of God bringing order to the brooding waters of primordial chaos. I knew my location for a brief moment. I quickly went to the chart table below and plotted a course for Redfish Island. I had navigated there often by eyeball but it was time to test my dead reckoning on this day of disorientation. If I did it right, I would raise the island in less than two hours. If I did it wrong, I would be completely lost. I turned *Moonghost* east-southeast on a blind course of 110 degrees.

Most of life is like that voyage. Not much happens. You just keep on keepin' on. There are anxious moments—"Am I on the right course with my life?" And there are moments of terror—" Is there something or someone out there, something I can't see, waiting to sink me?" And there are other moments of gentle triumph yielding the simple yet often illusory satisfaction that we have arrived at the very place that we expected to find.

I slowed to a half-knot and stood in the bow pulpit to scan what should have been the horizon. A dark shape was a few degrees to port. I must be nearing the island's north hook where an oyster shell beach extends several hundred yards to the west. I floated quietly for a few moments, relieved, and remembered a sunny spring day when I was anchored in this very spot while a pod of dolphins danced around me.

Life's familiar landmarks mask a deeper mystery. We drift on reality's surface while currents of truth move in the depths…. A misty puff from a dolphin's blowhole broke my reverie. I followed the sound to see four young dolphins leap across my bow, looking directly into my eyes before each dive. Their backs glowed a brilliant emerald color as they beckoned me to follow them.

My emerald guides slowly led me toward the shore. Amusement gave way to anxiety as the depth sounder warned of increasing shoaling: seven feet, then six, then five—soon I would have to stop or risk grounding. Just as I slowed the balky diesel to 900 rpm and started to shift into reverse, the readings changed: first to six feet, then to twenty, then to one hundred! A pass appeared in the beach—a pass I knew was not there. I followed the emerald dolphins into a lagoon more beautiful than any I had explored in the tropics. The water glowed with the same color as my dolphin guides. In a tropical anchorage, emerald water is about thirty feet deep but this lagoon didn't follow the ordinary laws of nature. The depth sounder had a total breakdown. This pool had no bottom!

I looked astern. The fog that had embraced *Moonghost* was now a gray wall on the far side of a low island that nearly surrounded me. We floated in an emerald pool of unknown depth. Soft warm light flowed upward over me and my boat.

I have anchored beside this island hundreds of times. I know the reef, and I know the bottom. I searched for predictable behavior in this new universe where the familiar was a gateway to mystery. I could relax if I could set my hook in the bay's mud bottom, have a boat drink, and enjoy this illusion. Life would return to normal, and I would simply be resting after a foggy voyage to a favorite spot. I motored to within ten feet of the beach and went forward to prepare the ground tackle.

"Don't," the voice said gently.

There could be no voice. No one was there.

"Don't. You don't need to, and you can't anyway. There's no bottom. Just leave her be. She won't go anywhere."

I saw him over my right shoulder, sitting quietly beside a driftwood fire. His skin was dark, perhaps black, perhaps sunburned, or perhaps Middle Eastern. He wore faded denim, old leather sea boots, and a torn Greek fisherman's cap. His eyes were small slits, creased by years at sea, and they glowed with the same soft light that permeated the lagoon and shone on the dolphins' backs: a light that came from within as though he and the light were one.

The fire offered welcome warmth after the damp voyage. After a silent moment, he asked, "Are you hungry? I'm baking some shrimp on the coals. Come and have breakfast."

Something about this scene was familiar as though I had read it somewhere. Something about this strange sailor was safe as though I had always known him. I nudged *Moonghost*'s bow near the shore, jumped off, and let her drift away. I liked the solid crunch of the shell beach under my feet. I liked the heat of the driftwood fire. And I liked my companion. "Who are you?"

"A sailor of truth," he answered, his eyes glowing a little brighter. "A voyager beyond the boundaries."

I felt a like a fish trying to resist the bait that floated in front of it. I had to ask, even though I knew that I would be hooked, "Where have you sailed? What ports have you visited?"

He began to spin stories. "I have sailed the deserts of Arabia, plied the Nile and the Tigris, crossed the Indian Ocean, and cruised the Sea of Japan...." He told of his travels and the people he had known. His adventures were like those of any seafarer but they seemed to mean more than the words he spoke, as though his words sounded more in my heart than in my ears. But of all his tales, those of the Middle East touched me most deeply. His last was of a mutiny: his crew deserted him and left him to die, tied high to the yardarms.

"How did you get out of that one?" I wondered.

"I didn't," he whispered in the solitude.

We sat in silence for weeks that day. The unspoken intimacy of an unexpected loving peace moved between our hearts while we watched the dolphins play in the lagoon's soft light. Full of shrimp, warmed by the fire, comforted by my companion, I looked at the wall of fog that surrounded me and felt no desire to set sail for home. I was already at home.

Finally I broke the silence. "What do you want of me?"

"I need your ship."

I froze. Was this man I had trusted really a pirate? Would I be marooned on this island?

"No," he somehow knew my fears. "No. I don't want to take anything from you. I want you to carry a cargo for me. You will find that it belongs to you as well. You have traveled with an empty hold for too long. You have found nothing worthy of your life's voyage. That's why you have come here today. That's why I brought you to this place. I have much to give you—gifts that you will carry back to your world. You will become richer than you have ever dreamed as you share them with others."

I hesitated. I was almost comfortable with the emptiness of my life. It was familiar. At least I knew what I *didn't* believe, and I believed a lot in not believing those things. It had taken a long and painful time to unload the cargo that others had dumped into me. I wasn't sure I wanted to take on anything new. I liked traveling light.

"Relax. My burden *is* light. You can carry it with ease on *Moonghost*. Others dumped tablets of stone into your hold. You were right to throw them overboard. You can throw my cargo overboard, too, if it turns to stone."

I was quiet for a long time. I walked away from the fire. I wanted to be alone. I looked at the wall of fog that stood between me and my familiar but empty world. Seagulls swept down to steal the shrimp tails that we had left on the beach. Shells crunched under the weight of my steps. The emerald-eyed sailor hunkered patiently by the fire.

I walked back. "Let's talk. I have room on *Moonghost* for your cargo."

CHAPTER 2

▼

CHRISTIANISM'S
BONES

I felt an unfamiliar peace with this disheveled sailor who knew more about my inner life than I did. He hardly resembled a respectable yacht club commodore in his tattered clothes, fisherman's boots, sweat-stained cap, and dark skin, yet I knew I could trust him. How, I wondered, did he know that my hold was empty?

I had been voyaging empty for a long time. Once I thought I knew what to pack in my sea bag. I had carried the formulas and creeds that others gave me. I had expected them to guide me but now they were useless relics that I no longer trusted. They might maroon me somewhere in the past. They could mislead me like outdated charts.

In the days of sailing ships, captains becalmed in tropical heat lightened their load. They knew that a less encumbered ship would respond to any ghost of breeze that touched it. Like them, I was becalmed on my soul's voyage. And I traveled ever lighter as I searched for the Spirit's movement. I had jettisoned most of the dogmas and doctrines that I once thought were essential by the time I left my slip on this foggy day.

"I know that," the sailor smiled.

"You know my thoughts?"

"I know your heart," he said. "I know that you sail aimlessly. I know that you are lost in fog. I know that your beliefs have died and you don't know how to replace them. That's why you are here."

My heart wept as his words touched me. They told me what I had feared to admit to myself: I was in the spiritual Horse Latitudes. No matter how much I threw overboard, the Spirit's whisper did not fill the sails of my soul. Sometimes I thought I could sense her breezes, like cat's-paws across the bay, but always they moved in another direction and left me to drift alone.

"You think too much," he grinned. "You think you can figure it out if you work on it. Give it up. No amount of analysis can resurrect what's rotten." He looked at the skeleton of a mullet lying on the beach. "Do you believe that you can make that mullet live again by analyzing its body parts and diagramming what they once did?"

"No," I stammered, wondering where he was leading me.

"Well, you can't do that with your lost beliefs either. You keep looking at their rotting skeletons and wonder why you don't see their beauty."

Now my eyes wept along with my heart. He knew my yearning. I had lost the spiritual security that I once possessed. I understood religion's illusions and cruelty. And I had not found anything to take its place.

"Your faith will heal you," he said gently. "It takes great faith to doubt so honestly."

He was too close too soon. I squirmed and looked away.

"There are many like you," he reassured me. "The soul's oceans swarm with solo sailors. Each thinks he or she is the only one out there. The truth is, there are enough of you to form a whole new fleet. You might as well do it: the old fleet's sinking fast. It's time for you to discover each other.

"Sit down by the fire. Open your mind, calm your heart, and listen. I'll tell you about a treasure hunter."

And so began the first of that afternoon's many parables....

Charlie knew *it* was somewhere in the Caribbean. The treasure was on a deserted island, beneath the white sand of a palm-bordered beach, in the ruins of an old sugar mill, or stashed in a dark sea cave. That treasure had inspired mariners for nearly two thousand years. It had inspired him. But he couldn't find it.

The treasure map was an exotic collection of ancient writings. Each fragment of the map told stories about others like him—stories full of intrigue, incest, murder, death, hope, community, and new life—stories that filled his heart. But characters in the stories possessed the treasure that eluded him.

Charlie read the map a thousand times. Each time he learned more about the treasure's beauty. It was like a diamond reflecting tropical sun, sparkling facets that waiting to be explored. The diamond called out to him. His heart would be restless until it was his own.

The map that so brilliantly described the treasure had lousy directions for finding it. Charlie wondered if those who copied the original had erased the instructions. His copy was made from millions of other copies. Maybe the keepers of the map wanted to control the treasure hunters by telling them of the diamond's beauty while they hid the key to finding it. He knew that the map-keepers had become a crusty and contentious group as the centuries passed. They dangled the map in the sight of generations of treasure hunters and offered to help them find its secrets but they exiled any who came close to the prize. The map-keepers promised much and delivered little.

Charlie's sloop, *Heart's Hunter*, reflected his simple lifestyle. An oar powered her when the wind died. An oaken bucket served as a head. Sails caught the rain to replenish his fresh water tanks. Meals were warmed over an alcohol stove. He had learned, as he read the stories in the map, that it's difficult to find the treasure if life is complicated.

Throughout many years of searching he had poked *Hunter's* bow into countless island coves. Steel bands serenaded him while he swung at anchor in gentle trade winds. Occasional hurricanes tested his skills. Beaches invited him to dig deeply for the treasure. Island girls tempted him to give up his search. But always his quest was unfulfilled, and he weighed anchor hoping that the treasure would be around the next point.

Sometimes he would sip rum late into the night at a beachfront bar. Other sailors spoke of their own searches. Some belonged to one of the map-keepers groups and argued that they knew the one true way to read the map's stories. Charlie always figured that they wouldn't argue so much if they had really found the treasure—they must be under the map-keepers' spell. Others, disillusioned with the map-keepers, traveled alone but still believed that they would find the treasure. And still others had stopped traveling altogether. They sat at the bar, played with their drinks, and tried to convince Charlie that the map was a lie: there was no treasure.

One night Charlie left the bar with a belly full of rum, walked past the old tire swing that hung from a bent palm tree, and stumbled into his dinghy. Countless drunken discussions about map-keepers had become empty rhetoric. Either there was a treasure or there wasn't, and he wasn't going to find the truth sitting in a bar. His heart grew confident as he rowed toward *Hunter*. This night he would follow his heart's lead.

It's dangerous to sail at night in tropical lagoons bordered by coral reefs. Charlie didn't care. If *Hunter* bumped a coral head and sank, he'd paddle back to the bar and join those who had given up. Tonight he had only one choice. He threaded his way through the reef into open water.

Charlie and *Hearts Hunter* sailed southeast, close-hauled in the moonlight, past countless small cays. His heart sang as he reached toward a mountainous island that rose before him. He could neither stop nor turn back: the treasure must be near! His heart was like a radio direction finder that guided him to a small sea-cave on the west side of the island. He memorized the cave's location as he sailed past and anchored in a secure bight protected from the trades. The time was full. If he didn't find the treasure in that cave, there would be no more searches.

Guided by dawn's subtle light, he rowed his dinghy around a rocky point toward the cave. His heart's shout deafened him to the surf's pounding: the treasure was here, waiting for him! Inside he saw a scene straight from a classic tale of piracy: a wooden chest, bound in leather straps, sitting on a ledge carved into the cave's stone wall.

Charlie sat on that ledge beside the treasure chest for a long time. He began to understand why people say that it's dangerous to find what you seek. Until now his life had been about searching. If this really were the treasure, then the search would be over. His life as he knew it would also be over, and his future course would be uncharted. Others had come to this point and turned back. They preferred the familiarity of their quest or the illusory security of the map-keepers' groups to the treasure's unknown promises.

Charlie's right hand played with the latch. His ambivalent mind mired itself in possibilities but his heart didn't hesitate. The hand opened the chest. The rest of his life would be shaped by what lay within it. Though his excitement was frosted with fear, he hadn't come this far only to return to the prison of his past. He scooted carefully over the damp rock, his feet hanging past the ledge to be tickled by waves that bumped his dinghy into the cave's wall, leaned over, and looked inside.

No sparkling diamonds gleamed at him. No gold trinkets trapped the dawn's sunlight. No jade statues tempted his vision. He saw only whitened bones and ragged scraps of decaying manuscripts. Shocked and dismayed, he sagged against the ledge. Could this chest full of death be what people have sought so desperately?

He looked again, listened to his heart, and understood. These are the bones of the map-keepers, and the papers are the guidance they erased from the map. His heart knew what his mind had not grasped: the death of those who control the treasure is itself a great treasure! With the death of the map-keepers comes great freedom for those who have the courage to accept it.

Excited now, he burrowed through the chest's rot and debris. Bones and scraps flew past his ears and still he dug like a dog looking for a deeply buried bone. Finally his fingernails scraped the bottom. He brushed aside the dust—there, lying face down, was an ordinary mirror, round, with a long handle. A greenish glow spread from its edges: the color of life in the midst of all the death the chest contained. His quivering hands raised the mirror and turned it over. The green light grew brighter until it filled the cave. Here, in the burial place of those who try to control honest seekers, was the treasure at last.

He looked into the mirror. A face looked back at him—a face strange yet familiar, the eyes of someone he had always known but did not yet know…. A breeze whispered from the mouth of the cave: "It is your original face. You are the treasure. The One who packed this chest, who carried it here, who buried it deep in this cave for you to find, that One loves you. That One treasures you. Your true self, your soul, is the treasure."

The old salt stood, brushed a shrimp hull off his left thigh, and stared at the south end of the island, "Let's do our own treasure hunting!" He grabbed my right hand and jerked me to my feet. I was a little dizzy. The story had stunned me with its whimsy and its gravity, like a lead balloon that somehow rose to the heavens. And now he wanted to hunt for treasure in this place? This island was just shell and driftwood. It held nothing of value.

"Look more deeply," he said. "There is no place that is not treasured. There are no valueless places in God's universes."

I spotted a small shovel by the fire. I don't know how it got there. I carried it as we walked along the shoreline's curve. Ahead of us, on the southern point, was a slight rise on the beach that I had never noticed in the hundreds of times I had come here. But then, the "here" that afternoon was an entirely different "here" than I had visited before. He walked a step ahead of me and stopped at the little mound.

"You dig," he grinned. "I'm old, and anyway, I already have my treasure. This one's here for you."

It wasn't easy cutting through the shell with a small shovel but the treasure chest wasn't buried very deep.

"It's always easy to find if you know where to look."

He was right. But, of course, I didn't know I was looking for it until that moment. I still wasn't sure that this was intended for me but I trusted this geezer for some reason. If he said I was looking for it, then I guess that's what I was doing.

We hoisted the old chest onto the beach, ran a couple of driftwood poles through its leather bindings, and hauled it back to the fire. By this time I knew that it had been buried there for me, like the treasure in the story, and that it carried truths that would set me free. I was a little anxious about what I might discover.

We lifted the lid together. The musty decay of old death momentarily filled the humid air of the lagoon. Was I Charlie in his Caribbean cave? Inside were the same broken decadent bones and aged scraps of paper. It was déjà vu all over again.

"I don't understand." I looked at my island host. "Is every treasure chest the same?"

"Every treasure chest contains what is needed for the hunter to discover the freedom and the truth of his or her deepest self. But, yes, for most honest seekers it is pretty much the same stuff. As the old saying goes, 'what is most personal is most universal.'"

I lifted the bones and stacked them on the beach. "What are they and whose are they?"

"They are the bones of Christianism," he answered.

I was confused again. I knew what Christianity was, or at least I knew as much as anyone about what it was supposed to be. But I had never heard of Christianism.

"These are the bones of spiritual constriction: of church leaders who have turned the freedom of Love's Spirit into a cult of religious correctness and creeds."

"Like Saul's assent to stone Stephan, and Samuel's dethronement of King Saul for his refusal to commit total genocide, and Calvin's approval of burning Servetus for his interpretation of the Trinity?"

"Yes, and many more. Those are the glaring grievances of these bones. But the worst crimes are against the minds and spirits of ordinary believers in ordinary churches."

I lifted another handful. "What of these?"

"These are the bones of political alliances: of leaders and movements that have tied Christ to the crosses of nationalism."

"Like Nazism and the 'American way of life'," I asked.

"Yes." His tone was somber. "Yes, and all the ways that the religious leaders through the centuries have traded faith for worldly power."

"That can be pretty subtle," I replied. "For a long time I wondered why my own denomination was more concerned with liberal causes than with helping people know Christ. Now I am beginning to understand...."

"There are as many ways to trade faith for power as there are leaders whose egocentric needs drive them to do it. There is a fine line between serving God in the political realm and serving yourself. Many have crossed it. You hold their bones."

I grabbed a handful of papers. The stiff dry parchment turned to dust in my hands. I let it trail in the wind and spread across the emerald water of the lagoon.

"And these?" I wondered.

"Those are the mystics' words hidden by church officials who ban what they can't control. Mystics are born of Spirit. Jesus described them best when he was talking to Nicodemus: 'you don't know where they're coming from or where they're going.' Mystics make religious powerbrokers sweat through their sheets at night. Your search is longer and more difficult than it might have been because anxious church leaders tore those papers from the map, your Bible."

I was beginning to understand what my new mentor meant by "Christianism." People like me once shared a wondrous experience of the risen presence of a man who was killed because he embodied God's love and freedom. Those people gave birth to a movement that promises everyone who struggles with negativity and death that God says "yes" to all of creation. But within a few generations that wonderful promise of new life was captured and controlled by doctrines and creeds and political power. In Christianism those who try to contain God and their disciples in tight theological, cultural, and political boxes persecute those who want to know God directly.

This was heavy stuff. I looked at the quiet water for a long time. I didn't want to believe that the beauty of Christ had died in the distortions of religion.

He read my thoughts again: "It hasn't. It will never die. The 'isms' of this world aren't strong enough to contain their founders. Buddhism doesn't contain the Buddha. Marxism doesn't contain Marx and his concern for those who are exploited by corporate and industrial systems. And Christianism is not strong enough to contain Jesus. Isms are frames put around mysteries to make them marketable and easily managed."

I had to face the truth about religion. I knew he was right. I had never found a church anywhere in all my soulful voyages that consistently, intentionally, and consciously embodied Love or enabled its members to follow a life of spiritual transformation. Everyone I knew who truly sought God and walked a path of spiritual growth was outlawed, ignored, or humorously tolerated.

"If Christianism is dead, what will happen to the Jesus-people? What are we to do?"

He laughed. "You worry too much. Spirit and truth won't die. If they have survived all these bones, they will survive anything.

"That's why you're here. Christianism died for you a long time ago. That's why you travel with an empty hold."

That was slight reassurance for my sudden existential anxiety. I mourned the comfort of the old ways even though they oppressed me. I needed something to hang onto, like a safety harness tethered to *Moonghost* when a sudden gale strikes. I knew other wandering sailors who had retreated into the harbors of their past and traded suppression for security. And I knew still others who tried new churches only to discover that the newness was superficial—they tied their members with the same old chains.

"Where do I go now?" I asked. "I need to believe something."

He shook his head in patient frustration. "You already do. You are a wandering Jesus-person in diaspora. There're many like you."

Charlie's story had one more piece. I wondered if mine did as well. I had found part of the treasure: the gift of spiritual freedom. But I felt a little anxious about that freedom. Too much freedom leaves me wondering if I am wandering aimlessly.

The Island Mystic smiled and nodded towards the chest: "Look inside. You need the rest of the treasure."

I scraped aside the dust. The mirror lay surrounded by the green light of life. I trembled.

"Pick it up."

I lifted it to my face with fear and trembling. Someone strange and familiar looked back at me. I studied the eyes of a person I had known all of my life, yet one I didn't really know.

"That's the tether of your safety harness," the sailor comforted me. "You are God's treasure. You don't know your true self, your soul. That knowledge is the destination of your voyage. So remember this: when you sail in freedom, you also sail in Love's presence. The treasure you have sought is the heart of God. *God treasures you.* Remember always: where God's heart is, there is the treasure."

I'd never thought of it that way. I guess I was clinging to some old shame imposed by the map-keepers. They taught me that I was a sinner, that I was totally depraved, and that I was unlovable. It would take awhile to digest this new view of myself. But I liked what I was learning.

My friend looked sternly at me. "Listen! This is the first cargo for your empty hold: you sail in freedom, and Love saves you in the storms."

"But," I argued, "this kind of freedom doesn't teach me much about discerning the truth. How will I know the truth when I see it? I don't want the oppressors of Spirit to capture me again."

He laughed loudly. "Funny you should ask that! Sit down and I'll tell you about truth and discernment."

CHAPTER 3

▼

TRUTH DIVING

Sam learned the hard way that Mulder had been wrong from the beginning. All those T-shirts warning, "The truth is out there," were lies. The truth is not "out there." The truth, Sam discovered, is *down there*.

Sam didn't always know that. For most of his life, like everyone else, he believed that "the truth was out there." In the Florida Keys "out there" meant the ocean. The truth must be somewhere on the surface of the sea. If he just looked hard enough and long enough, it would show up.

But it didn't.

Other people claimed to find it. They searched deserted debris-choked beaches and found dead fish washed up by idle tides. In their desperate eyes those rotting pieces of rotting reality were revelations that had the power to save their lives. But truth based on dead fish never made much sense to Sam. Anything that stunk didn't have much beauty about it. "Surely," he thought, "the truth must be beautiful."

Sam's enlightenment happened like this....

Every day Billy walked the windward sands of the small key where he lived. There wasn't much else to do. He had lost the job of his dreams where his profession had become his art: the wonder of swirled ice cream at the local Dairy Queen. No one else on the island could swirl like Billy. And then, one day, when Billy had built an especially beautiful cone and dipped it deep into liquid chocolate, he didn't feel his usual passion. His heart melted faster than ice cream in the tropical heat.

Sweat soaked Billy in the artificial coolness of the Dairy Queen. For the first time in his simple life he felt the angst of existential crisis. Swirling had lost its meaning. He tried to find the same sense of purpose in French fries, but they were empty. Burgers didn't work either. His heart hungered for nothing on the Queen's menu.

Billy's boss wanted happy customers, not a moody clerk who served frowns and droopy cones. Within a week Billy became a starving ice-cream artist. He wandered tropical sands, depressed and lost in his grief. He didn't know any scriptures that would help him in his despair, but he remembered a T-shirt that inspired him, "The Truth is Out There," worn by a chunky dishwater blond who ordered onion rings. Every day he looked for the truth in the ocean and the refuse it flung on the beach, but nothing spoke to him. "Maybe," he wondered, "the T-shirt was wrong. Maybe there ain't no truth out there anywhere." The thought was too much for him; in fact, most thoughts were too much for him.

Billy was afraid that it was too late. His spirit was dead. He turned to the east, to the ocean from whence he once hoped his help would come. No longer caring, no longer searching, he slowly walked towards France. He figured his troubles would end before he got there. But Billy couldn't even do suicide right. He stumbled on his way to death and flopped face-down in a murky tidal pool.

Suddenly, there *it* was. He'd often heard that you had to hit bottom before you could be saved. He lay there, on the bottom of the pool and of his life. Before him was his salvation, the very thing that had prevented his death. *It* was a dead Mahi Mahi.

"I'm saved," Billy shouted. And he kept shouting it the rest of the day. He picked up that stinking carcass, slung it over his shoulder like the good shepherd once bore a lamb, and headed for town. "I'm saved! I'm saved!"

There were lots on lost souls on that little key. Some of them heard Billy's shouts of joy. They spilled out of the bars and the crack houses and pursued him and his savior down the street. This truly was a revelation. It was *the* truth. Soon a parade of losers, scoundrels, and tourists trailed Billy as he shouted, "You too can be saved! The kingdom of the Ocean is at hand. Follow the Mahi Mahi!"

And so they followed as blindly and aimlessly as Billy led. He took them into his home, a mosquito-infested shack on the edge of a mangrove swamp. They watched as he mounted the dead fish, flies and all, above his fireplace. The crowd soon spilled onto his weed-littered lawn. Billy knelt before the fish. They knelt. He lit a candle, and soon the whole yard looked like a convention of fireflies.

Word quickly spread that the truth really was *out there.* Other empty hearts took to the beach to find their own revelations.

Sally sought the sacred tidal pool. She wanted to wash herself in its slimy salvation. Perhaps she, too, would receive a revelation. She had been alone and lonely since her no-good drunken husband beat her, spent the rent money, and ran off with his transsexual lover. She refused to blame him for her emotional pain. Now she had no one to fight with, no one to reject when he wanted to have sex, and no one to hate. What good is life when you have no one to make you suffer?

Lost in memories of sweet nights of battered love, Sally slipped on a beached and decaying marlin and fell facedown into a new life. A *marlin*!!! A major revelation!

Sally grabbed her savior's tail and dragged its hulk of rotting flesh back to town. Her screams were a litany that proclaimed to all on the street that she had found more truth, bigger truth, truer truth, than Billy's sacred *mahi mahi.* A band of angry singles followed her to her home where she hung the marlin in a tree. There, too, the faithful lit candles and knelt in prayer.

Roger didn't trust the saltwater cults. He believed in the truth of dead fish. He believed that you didn't have new life until you were baptized in a slimy pool. But Roger was a rebel. After all, he had always lived as a free man: he smoked when he was only twelve; used pot at fourteen; had sex at fifteen (although, in that town, it wasn't clear whether it was with a woman); and wrecked four cars at sixteen. Yes, Roger was a free thinker.

And Roger knew there was something fishy about saltwater salvation. The truth couldn't be found in something so sticky and messy. The truth would come only from the divine righteousness of pure fresh water. The truth must be found on a lake.

So Roger gassed up his bass boat, donned his camouflage jump suit, grabbed a handful of plastic worms, and set out on his own vision quest. He didn't know much about catching fish but he had read a lot of old sportsmen's magazines in the barbershop, and he knew that the most important fish were found dead on the shoreline. His boat screamed across the swampy lake toward some old stumps where bass were sure to hide. He figured that when they died they would float to a nearby shore.

Of course, plastic worms aren't much good for catching dead fish, but that thought never crossed Roger's mind. He was on a quest for truth, and thinking was not part of the program. The far shore drew closer and Roger's grin grew wider. It was *out* there, *over* there, and soon would be his. He closed his eyes and dreamed of his fame as a televangelist—faithful viewers across the nation trained on him as he stood, in white suit and camouflage tie, proclaiming the freshwater gospel of bass.

Roger's reverie was shattered by the giant sucking sound of his boat's hull on soft mud. The boat stopped, but Roger didn't. He soared gracelessly across the bow and onto the muddy shore. He tried to smile as the silty water lured him into consciousness: "I'm saved. I'm baptized. And this is *fresh* water." (It smelled more like an open sewer.) He rubbed his face and wondered why his mouth felt funny, then looked at his hands. "Funny," he mused, "I know I don't brush every day, but I don't remember having scales on my teeth." He rubbed again, then knew that the rotting largemouth bass of truth was stuck securely on his incisors.

Soon religious wars broke out on Sam's little island. There was a schism between followers of the Marlin and the mother church of the *Mahi Mahi*. Months later, a reform movement began that historians would call the Freshwater Reformation. Roger's Bass was the first icon of the new faith, but splinter groups found truth in Bluegills, in Perch, and in Catfish. Some turned to the dark side, embracing the gothic anti-truth of Stingrays. Every car on the island displayed its own plastic dead fish on the rear bumper. Pilgrims flocked to the local bars, took in the sights, and sat in awed silence before their chosen carcass.

Sam's skepticism grew with the movement. Jaded, cynical, and full of boat drinks, one night he declared himself an a-ichthyist. Every waterfront has a Shipwreck Bar. Sam's shipwrecked life had washed up on a shoreline covered with dead fish and crazy people.

"Don't," he heard.

"Don't what?" Sam turned to see a sailor on the next barstool. His age was ageless. His eyes had a weird crystal emerald glow that shone through sun-baked skin. This man had been around a long time—maybe had circumnavigated more than this world.

"Don't give up looking for the truth."

Sam scratched the stubble on his face and took another drink. "It's not out there. And it's not dead fish. These people are nuts. How can you say you know the truth if you hate everyone who disagrees with you? I mean, holy crabcakes, maybe there isn't any way to know it."

The emerald eyes looked deeply into Sam like an x-ray of his soul: "You can't know it *that* way. Truth isn't out there and it's not something that you can pick up and carry around. It's not in the scriptures of the Marlins or the Bass, and it's not dead. You can't nail truth to the wall or hang it on a tree."

"Well," Sam drawled, "if it's not out there, where the devil is it? It ain't at Dairy Queen, it ain't at Roger's place, and it ain't in Sally's swamp, so where is it?"

"The truth," slowly the sailor's words pierced Sam's thoughts, "is *down there.*"

"Down there?"

"Yes. It's down there. You will find it when you go as deep as you can, and when you find it, you will know that you can't frame it, stuff it, or capture it in sacred fishing magazines."

Sam had been diving most of his life. He knew the reefs around his island better than his own backyard. He had found beauty and danger there, but he had never seen the truth.

"Deeper," the sailor's voice echoed silently in his mind.

Deeper, Sam knew, was beyond the wall, where the bottom fell to over six thousand feet. It was impossible to go past one hundred feet. It was death to try diving down the wall.

"Go look anyway," the voice whispered.

Visions of the abyss beyond the wall assaulted Sam's sleep that night—the abyss where a diver could sink forever, squeezed by the ocean's black hole into a speck of food for unknown denizens. *It* couldn't be down there. Nothing was down there where even light couldn't penetrate. And he sure as hell didn't want to be part of that darkness....

But sometimes you can only see light when the darkness is complete....

Sam broke all the rules when he made this dive. He went without a buddy or a safety net. His search was solitary. He gave no one his dive plan. Maybe everyone has to do this sooner or later, but Sam couldn't imagine Roger or Billy or Sally or the congregating crews of the dead fish cults ever standing alone on the shore. He thought that the whole idea behind the dead fish movement was to ensure that its crewmembers could avoid this dive. But Sam had to do it. The old sailor at the Shipwreck Bar made sure of that.

He trembled as he pulled on his dive skins, buckled his weight belt, and attached his buoyancy compensator to the air tank. He reset his dive computer, strapped a knife to his calf, pulled his mask and snorkel over his head, slipped into his fins, and backed through the shore break into deep water. His favorite reef lay a hundred yards offshore, and beyond it was the abysmal wall. Sam was at home, swimming now in water forty feet deep. Yellowtail snappers played with him, a big grouper led the way, and a stingray flew slowly to his left. Fan coral waved with the quiet current and parrotfish nibbled at dead staghorn branches. The light was bluer, calmer, cooler, and a familiar peace flooded Sam. "Maybe this peace is the truth. Maybe it really *is* down here." And then the sailor's voice prodded him,

"Farther down, Sam, deeper and deeper. If you think you have found it, you haven't."

Sam paddled to the edge of the reef. He shuddered as he looked down the wall, past the familiar ridges and valleys, into nothingness. The light grew dimmer as he descended, and he used his dive light to look at giant tube sponges and brain corals that grew from the side of the cliff. He watched his dive computer and depth gauge: eighty, ninety, a hundred feet. This was as far as he could go, and still he didn't see the truth. The old sailor was probably some kind of nut, and so was he for believing him!

And then: the change was subtle, almost indiscernible, but clearly something was there. Out of the darkness thousands of feet below, a quiet glow appeared like a sea buoy on a night passage, pulsing then disappearing. Fish swimming up from the depths carried that same glow, losing it as they swept towards the surface. Sam had found what he sought. He could not see it clearly, he could not describe it, and he could not take it home to show others. He felt a profound sense of peace, of love, and of awe as he watched the fish ascend and descend like Jacob's angels. This was not a beach covered with rotting dead fish. This was a place of life, of beauty, and of love.

Sam couldn't remain at this depth. He needed at least twenty minutes of air to make a safe ascent. His heart glowed with the same light that illuminated the fish as he drifted up the wall, swam across the reef, and walked thoughtfully back to the shore.... What could he tell others? Only that the truth is alive and beautiful, not dead and rotting; that the truth can be glimpsed but not grasped; and that the truth brings peaceful love, not division and conflict. He carried his heavy gear back to his cabin with a light and hopeful heart. Others returned from the sea with death and illusions. He returned with life and joy. Others nailed their catch to the wall. He nailed a sign to his front door: "Truth Diving—I can teach you how, but you have to do it alone."

I looked at the stranger on the beach. Dew dripped from my hat and sizzled on the driftwood fire. He tossed a few more shrimp on the coals.

"Was that you?" I wondered. And "wonder" was truly the right word. Even more than when I sailed into this mystical lagoon, I was overcome with confusion.

"Could be," he grinned, and his emerald eyes glistened.

I was beginning to understand a little bit of the cargo he wanted me to carry away in *Moonghost*. Maybe he didn't want the cargo in my boat at all. Maybe he wanted it inside me: "You want me to carry the truth back to shore?"

"Nope. You can't do that. If you think you can carry the truth to anyone, then you don't understand the story. You've got to make your own dive, and when you do, then you can't pin what you find to your living room wall for others to worship. They've got to strap on their own tanks and get wet before they can know the truth."

"I think I'm beginning to get it," I answered.

"Be careful," he warned, "because if you think you've got it, you don't, but you must believe that you have it even when you know you can't have it."

My mind spun circles around that last one. We sat for a long time while the shrimp cooked. I tossed another piece of wood on the fire: "Tell me. I don't always get it."

He looked sharply through the drifting smoke. "You're a little slow, aren't you? I'll try to make it plain, but it fits a lot better in a story. Folks like you have caused no end of trouble trying to make it plain. But listen...."

And he began to explain things. The best I can remember is that he said something like this: "What we know is like the ocean. Most of it is on the surface, and it changes almost daily. A philosopher once said that a fact is what everybody agrees is true, so facts change when we change our minds. The changes in physics are like that. Your culture's understanding of truth is changing as people shift from Newtonian to quantum models of reality. They're all on the surface, but people cling to them as though they were the *last* word about truth, when they really are just the *latest* word. By the time most people think about it their version of truth is as dead as those rotting fish on the beach.

"People's ideas, which live and die like fads, are not *the* truth. They are *truths*, and truths change. Truths' lives are short, like those fish. People fight and die over 'truths,' only to learn in the next generation that their truths are no longer true. Dead truths are like dead fish: they rot, they stink, they make people sick, and they are mostly illusions.

"You can't know much of the truth with your left-brain. You can't know much of it logically, and you can't prove it with science. But you can glimpse it, love it, and appreciate its beauty. You can find things that point to it like those glowing fish that came from the depths, but be careful not to mistake the pointers for the reality they point to."

I listened, sweating in the cold dampness. Something about what this man said made me anxious: "It doesn't sound like anything is really true. Nobody's going to buy that. It doesn't leave us anything to believe in."

He smiled patiently. "It gives you everything to *trust*. It just doesn't leave you in control of things. The truth isn't relative. The truth is absolute. You can trust it completely, and it won't make you anxious. It always brings peace and compassion to the consciousness of all who *relate* to it."

"Relate to it?"

"Yes. That's how you know truth—not like knowing that two and two are four, but by having a relationship with it. And then you can help others find the way to have that same kind of relationship. But be careful. Hold onto your truths very lightly for fear that you might mistake them for truth."

In the world beyond the wall of fog, people didn't know things by having relationships with them. They knew things by thinking about them. This salty stranger was saying that I needed a different kind of mind if I was going to know what was really true. My old way of thinking wouldn't work in this lagoon.

"How can I know by relating?"

"Have you ever heard the saying, 'the truth shall make you free?'"

"Yes. Jesus said it, and people quote it all the time."

"No," he gently chided me, "people *mis*quote it. People think that it means that anything that seems true will set them free. But that isn't how it works. Do you remember what else he said about truth?"

"Yes. He said that he is the truth."

The stranger smiled. "Yes, and he's a person. He's not a dead fish, not a set of ideas, and not a collection of rules. To know the freedom of truth, you have to know him as a person. And most people would rather collect dead fish. They would rather know *about* him."

I was silent, and the stranger waited. "I want to dive into this more deeply."

Again he smiled patiently. "He's on the cargo list, but it's not yet time to talk about him."

"Why not? What comes next, if not him?"

"Well," he said, "if you want to talk about truth, you had better start with God."

I hesitated. "For a lot of people, God's a dead fish on religion's beach."

CHAPTER 4

▼

THE MASTER'S LUNCH

I munched on a shrimp and tossed the tail toward the lagoon. An emerald mullet caught it before it touched the water. I wasn't sure I wanted to get into this God business. I'd left my moorings looking for solitude, and the fog had seemed like a good place to find it. Now I was stuck on a reef with an ocean-going guru who spun metaphysical yarns about truth and its offspring. But something about the guy held me to the beach. I couldn't make myself leave, and, really, I didn't know how to do it anyway. Until the dolphins showed up or the fog lifted, I wasn't going anywhere.

He looked into my eyes and through my soul. "You're right. People want a god they can control, and define, and kill for, so they can stick knives into the souls or bodies of those who don't believe in their pet deity. That kind of god rots and makes the spiritual atmosphere stink.

"But dead gods aren't God anyway. To know God we have to give up God. Listen…."

The master's bare feet flew across the granite foothills of Mount Sinai. His disciples dragged far behind, moaned, complained, took deeper breaths, and struggled to keep him in sight. "Nobody said that enlighten-ment was easy," they grumbled, "but who thought it included cross-coun-try marathons."

The master smiled. Physical workouts had great value for spiritual endurance. His disciples griped about their journeys, but they would soon learn the great maxim of all the world's teachers: *no grumbling, no growth.* Love isn't easy. It always requires sacrifice. How can these disciples learn to sacrifice their egocentric selfishness if they don't sacrifice a little sweat and put up with a few cramped calf muscles? The master wasn't sadistic. While he didn't enjoy their pain, he delighted in their dedication.

And it *had* been a tortuous trek so far. There was a lot of desert still to cross before they left Mecca behind and rested in Jerusalem. And then there awaited an ocean passage to the Vatican, a bicycle trip to Calcutta, a secret passage into Tibet, and a flight to the sacred *sanctuario* at Chimayo. Along every road, he knew, the disciples would wonder why spiritual insight can't be found someplace that wasn't blistering with heat or frozen in thin atmosphere. "But," he smiled once more, "what better conditions to teach that the inner landscape is more formidable than the outer one?"

His smile faded. His feet hurt. His stomach rumbled. A powerful insight flickered from deep within his spiritual self and flashed across his ego's screen: even masters are human, and they get hungry! He remem-bered that there is no spirituality without incarnation, smiled to his empty gut, sat on a dusty rock in the shade of a scrubby tree, attended to his breath, and waited for his disciples to arrive. "Oh, what joy in simple breath," he mused, "yet breath is not enough to satisfy me.

"Nobody can live by breath alone.

"Sometimes I've got to eat peanut butter!"

Theirs was a search for God like every journey that's worth taking. You can't find God in Mecca, Jerusalem, the Vatican, Calcutta, Tibet, or Chi-mayo if you can't find God while you're taking a shower or paying bills. The only reason to take a journey to the sacred places of the world is to learn to recognize the sacred places inside of you. But, like most people, the disciples didn't know that. They were convinced that God was hidden and that God had a special love for inconvenience, physical suffering, poor air conditioning, and bad food. The master dragged them around the world to help them discover that they don't need to go anywhere but into a quiet room in their own homes.

That's the way it is when someone searches for God. The master knew this as he sat on the rock early in the trek. When his disciples knew it, they wouldn't need him anymore. But they didn't know it yet, as they straggled to sit around his feet in the hot dust. The motley mix of men and women carried heavy packs of food but their souls were fueled by the energy of hungry hearts. The master, they knew, would show them the secrets of God.

Their questions flew in every quiet moment. Is God Jewish or Muslim? Is she a Hindu goddess or serene Buddha? Is he/she Native American? Is God a New Age alien from Pleiades? Is God a vague mystical fog?

The master breathed: "what joy in simple breath," and let the questions float upward in the torrid air. He smiled at his followers and spoke. This was a big deal. His words were of great value because there weren't very many of them. "Fix me a peanut butter sandwich. Then I will tell you about God."

Nothing whomps up bedraggled disciples faster than their master's borborygmus.

Flower had been knocking around the seeker's circuit since Haight Ashbury in 1967, where she stepped from a trolley to receive the wisdom of a shaggy stranger: "Enjoy your now. That's all there is." He faded into the crowd. She's been fading ever since.

Once Flower's hope bloomed brightly: a new world was coming where peace was normal, wars were obsolete, sex was free, the air was clean, and everyone played in the park on sunny days. But her dreams found their way to the same garbage heap where all utopias go to die. Wars still kill thousands. Sex can cost your life. People work hard and don't make time to play in parks. In her heart, though, Flower nursed the same spark of hope that drove her to San Francisco for the "summer of love." Though life had taught her that utopia is nowhere, she understood that nowhere is "now-here." And something about "now" kept nagging at her. A sense, a presence, a hunch fed her dream.

The master didn't say much, but he smiled a lot. His childlike humor fanned the spark in her heart. She followed him into this desert. She planned to follow him to Tibet, India, Italy, and America—to follow him until utopia's now-here became somewhere. And she was delighted to fix a peanut butter sandwich for him.

Flower slowly unfolded from her lotus position. Thirty years of searching had kept her body as supple as her mind. She pushed back her hair to cool her face, hair now gray and matted that once hung to her waist with straight California blond freedom. She fluffed her dress, a natural wool that she wove herself. She had found the fleece in the Australian outback where she learned the spiritual secrets of aboriginal shamans. The dress captured her persona: natural, worn and tattered, yet functional and still hopeful.

As her aboriginal master had taught a decade past, Flower gathered dry leaves and sticks as fuel for a "natural" fire without the violence of matches. When the tinder began to smolder, she drew from her pack the ingredients of a truly organic peanut butter sandwich: whole wheat flour that she had ground herself during a harvest in eastern Montana; fresh organic peanuts (which she would grind into butter between two stones) that she had dug on Jimmy Carter's farm in Georgia; and pesticide-free bananas picked for her by friends in the Brazilian rainforest. She kneaded the flour into the shape of a bagel and smiled inwardly: her love for the master was the essential seasoning in this sandwich.

And the master smiled as well: "It is good that I find joy in simple breathing because it may be a long time before I eat."

Chris was the new kid on the seeker's block, fresh from Wall Street. His thousand-dollar suit spoke of frantic day trading and a successful career managing a mutual fund. Chris drove a Honda four-wheeler and towed a trunk that contained seven identical suits, ten pairs of hiking shoes (low tops with wingtips) from Eddie Bauer, a Palm Pilot with GPS, a laptop computer, and a satellite phone that kept him in constant contact with his banker on Grand Cayman Island.

Chris never thought about God before he signed up for the master's expedition. He did what was expected of a person in his position. He gave to charities, a not-very-selfless act that reduced his tax bill; took his trophy wife to fundraising balls; and was a deacon at his church where he served as director of the parking lot ministry. He thought that the church was good for the community, a fine place for kids to learn morals, with lots of opportunities for business networking. Recently Chris began to wonder why he was still in the Arabian Desert. He thought his travel agent had booked him on a trendy low-altitude Himalayan hike through Nepal. The master had assured him that they would go to the Himalayas as soon as they passed other mountains named Sinai, Olive, and Dome of the Rock. Chris had considered dropping out, but something about this man and these people nibbled at the walls around his heart. Besides, this was more fun than counting money.

Chris was thirsty and tired. If the master was hungry, then it was time to eat. He pushed his goggles to his forehead, spun to the left of his four-wheeler's saddle like a cowboy in the old West, and slid to the dusty hot sand. Straightening his suit, his oxford-cloth shirt, and his silk power tie, he turned to the trunk that trailed behind him, pushed a button on the top, and waited for a small satellite antenna to flip into position. He then toggled a Bluetooth switch on his cell phone that connected it to the antenna. While Flower made her bagel and ground her peanuts, he called the airport in Cairo. Soon a helicopter sliced through the desert heat. It carried his contribution to the master's lunch, chunky peanut butter on a Kaiser roll with grape jelly. It also carried a filet mignon, medium rare, and a liter of Glenlivet for his own lunch. Chris didn't believe that spirituality should include unnecessary sacrifice.

Bill was a nice guy. He liked Chris' eccentric and exaggerated sense of style but eschewed it for himself. He liked Flower's soulful dedication to her quest but knew he would never be a very good Hippie. Only Bill's gentle sincerity distinguished him. His heart was strangely moved when he heard the master's request for lunch. He rose, swept the dust from his Gap Easy-Fit jeans, stomped his worn-out New Balance jogging shoes, and shuffled away from the shade to the place where he had dropped his pack. Bill was nothing if not loyal. He would follow the master until he learned exactly who God is, just as he had always followed his parents' advice. He was their "good" child, the one who never gave them any trouble. This journey with the master was Bill's first adventure away from home.

Home: the thought of it haunted Bill. Home, with its air-conditioning, its soft firm bed and familiar worn sheets, its television, and his mother's cooking. Home, where he could taste love in every bite of food. Bill knew that the master had no home, no place to lay his head, and no mother to feed him. He resolved to give the master what they both were missing.

Bill's mother always used a special recipe for peanut butter sandwiches: smooth peanut butter without preservatives, mayonnaise instead of jelly, and soft white bread—and she always wiped the knife across the top of the sandwich when she finished making it. Bill rifled through his pack until he found his solar powered cooler and began to make the peanut butter delight of his natal table.

Sam yearned for the dampness of the keys. The desert's forlorn waste reminded him of the open ocean, but at least the ocean had life underground. Under the Sinai sand was more sand. He wanted to go truth diving, away from the heat where he could find the peace that always rose from the depths. All he could do in this (apparently) Godforsaken place was put one foot in front of the other and remember the cool Caribbean depths he had left behind.

As he trudged through the desert, Sam's mind wandered back to the beach where he had started his first truth dive. The heat pounded his head, but his thoughts played along the reef. Thus dissociated, he moseyed behind the others, immune to their ecology, until he bumped into Chris' parked trailer.

"What's going on?"

"The master wants a peanut butter sandwich," the others shouted in unison.

"So he shall have it!" Sam replied. He found a jar of the chunky stuff deep within his North Face pack. Digging still deeper, he scrounged some strawberry jam. Another layer yielded a few slices of whole wheat bread. And at the bottom was an empty jar. Carefully, mindfully, Sam spread the chunks across the bread and slathered them with jam. His masterpiece's bouquet filled him with olfactory delight. "Surely this is what the master needs: not the sandwich itself, but the essence of peanut butter, something he will remember the way I remember diving. He can save it for days of fasting. It will help him through that ordeal as memories of the reef have helped me in the desert."

Sam waved the empty jar across the aromatic cuisine three times. He slammed on the lid. And he wolfed down the sandwich.

After several hours the master called his disciples to him and smiled.

Flower laid her creation at his feet, a whole-wheat bagel cooked over a non-violent fire, loaded with hand-ground peanut butter, and tastily topped with a pate of gently softened rainforest bananas.

In a noisy whirl, the Cairo chopper dropped Chris' creation by parachute. Chris laid it at the master's feet: chunky peanut butter on a Kaiser roll, garnished with grape jelly, and served with a snifter of mellow Glenlivet.

Bill humbly approached the master. Shoulders hunched as his grateful tears spotted the sand, he studied the pebbles while he walked. He laid his gift before the master without lifting his eyes: mother's peanut butter and mayonnaise sandwich with a wipe-mark across the top.

Soon the pile of sandwiches reached the sky, bearing all manner of peanut butter: natural, preserved, low fat, smooth, chunky, chocolate silk, and cinnamon; all seasoned with grape jelly, strawberry jam, natural mayonnaise, preserved mayonnaise, apple butter, honey, creamed cheese, American cheese, and bananas; and all spread across various deli rolls, biscuits, tortillas, French bread, French toast, and bagels made of wheat, oats, and rye.

Sam emerged from his interior diving, the last disciple to make his offering, shook the ocean from his mind, and walked toward the sandwich tower. His flip-flops slapped the sand. On the very top, wary of tipping the whole thing over, he reverently put his jar of *eau de essence de pbj*.

The master smiled. "Which of these," he asked his disciples, "is *really* a peanut butter sandwich?"

"All of them," they answered, though some secretly believed that their own offerings were more sincerely authentic than the others.

"And which of them," he asked once more, "completely and totally and without reservation fully defines the essence of a peanut butter sandwich."

"None of them," the disciples responded sheepishly.

"Soon I shall tell you about God," the master said, "but first we shall eat."

When the tower of sandwiches left only a small shadow in the light of the setting sun, the master rose to speak: "No matter how many peanut butter sandwiches you make, you will never create their quintessence.

"So it is with God. Men and women are hungry for God. They create religious sandwiches seasoned with a little Mohammed, or some Jesus, or some Krishna, and perhaps a little Buddha, and they think they've got it. But they don't. They've got some of it, but no one has God's quintessence.

"Look on the master's lunch and learn."

The old sailor looked at me. "Do you remember the peanut butter sandwiches your own mother made?"

"Yes. They were a little like Bill's. She made them with Miracle Whip and white bread."

"Do you remember what you thought the first time you ate one that was different?"

"Yes. I was eight years old, at my next-door neighbor's house. His mother made a peanut butter sandwich with strawberry jam."

"And what did you do?" he asked.

I was beginning to get it. "I didn't want to eat it. It was strange. I didn't think it was a *real* sandwich. I didn't even like it. How could *anyone* eat jelly on a sandwich?" I knew then where he was leading me. I was raised a

Christian. For a long time, I thought being a Christian was the only way to know God. Christians even said that what Jesus meant when he said "no one comes to the Father except through me" was really "no one comes to the Father unless he or she accepts all the doctrines of the Christian church."

"It's OK," the sailor replied to my thoughts, "to like one kind of peanut butter sandwich more than another. Just remember, they all *must* have one thing in common: they must all have peanut butter in them so they all appeal to the taste of a genuine peanut butter lover."

"You are saying, aren't you, that every approach to God must have God as the basic ingredient?"

"Yes." He smiled like the desert master. "There is one essential ingredient that must be part of every approach to God. It seems kind of obvious, but religious people forget it. Every approach to God *must* appeal to the lover of God; otherwise, it won't feed a hungry heart. People can disagree about the bread and the spread, but not about that one ingredient."

"Is that what Jesus was trying to say?"

"Listen."

And then he was silent.

CHAPTER 5

▼

THE EXPLODING
HEART

The old sailor looked up. I followed his gaze to the fire's trail of smoke. Clouds that once covered us were gone. The circle of fog led upward, seemingly infinitely, into the kind of rich deep blue I have seen in desert mountains. I didn't know how the clouds could suddenly disappear yet the fog remain but by this time I had stopped disbelieving. Anything could happen on this afternoon.

He lifted his hand and pointed. A serene frigate bird soared far above us, perhaps two hundred yards into that beautiful sky. Our conversation about God wasn't over, and I didn't know what this pause for bird watching had to do with anything. But he was looking so I looked with him.

The bird adjusted its wings perfectly to hover above us in the sea breeze. It turned its head slightly, to look both left and right as though the fog existed only around this island while the sea beyond us was a normal hunting ground, then peered down through the tunnel of cloud to see us beside the fire, shrimp tails scattered about us, dolphins playing in the emerald lagoon, and *Moonghost* drifting nearby free from an anchor's tether.

"What do you know about the magnificent frigate bird?" He weighted his words more heavily than the question required and waited for my answer.

"I know nothing scientific," I said. "I don't know anything about the bird except the mythology blue water sailors give it." One of my life's greatest dreams was to be a blue water sailor. I had visions of myself encrusted with the salt of seven seas, drinking rum by a swimming pool at some distant marina, my trusty craft moored just inside the reef, as I told crowds of eager novices (and their bikini-clad crews) of my adventures around Cape Horn and the dangers of Tahiti's coral. But I never lived the dream. I sailed the bay, listened to Jimmy Buffett songs, and read magazines and books about cruising. I was an armchair sailor of the South Seas. I had learned about the mythology of frigate birds one winter sitting by the fire reading Slocum's *Sailing Alone around the World*.

I knew only one thing about them. Intuition told me what the island's mystic was looking for: "They are signs of hope. Frigate birds glide for hundreds of miles from shore. When a sailor has been at sea for weeks and spots a frigate bird he knows that land cannot be more than a few days away."

"Yes," my companion said, grinning slightly through his emerald eyes. "Hope. Hope for those who are afraid they are lost. Hope for those who seek shelter. Hope for those who explore new territory beset by the anxiety of the unknown. Hope for those who expect that death is the next port of call."

I was beginning to understand why a conversation about God was turning into a bird watching tour.

"You know, don't you," he asked, "that anything in the universe becomes a word of God when you know how to pay attention. If you have found your true eyes, you can see, and if you have found your true ears, you can hear."

I thought of my sons. When they were little they learned to find their noses and ears and eyes. And then I thought of how we forget to find them when we grow up. We become blind and deaf, anxious and grasping and ignorant. I looked again at the magnificent bird soaring in the heavens. I was ready to listen for a word....

"I would look like an immense frigate bird, as I soar above the sea through cloudless tropical skies. I would look exactly that way," mused Spirit, "but there is no one and nothing to see me."

Spirit soared above waters that existed only in her infinite imagination. The wind that carried Spirit was his own breathless breathing. There was nothing. There was no one. There wasn't even vast emptiness because emptiness requires a boundary of fullness. There was only Spirit and imagination. In the playful expanses of her heart's mind, Spirit could see the "might be" and the "could be" and the "isness" of all that was potential. But he could not see the "will be." The future was not yet present and the present could not fade into the past. All Spirit could know was *now*. And in *now* everything that could be, including the past and future, stood beside itself in completion.

Spirit's heart sometimes felt as empty as her mind felt full. "What is the good of imagining all that could be," she mused, "if I remain alone and unknown?"

Spirit had a name. He knew that a name should express the essence of the thing that carried it. She knew that because she was the one who had invented names. Her imagination was full of names like "dog," "quark," and "Sam." But there was no dog or quark or Sam for him to love. The only reality that Spirit could love was herself.

"I would say that loving me is getting old," she thought, "but there's no one to say it to. And it can't get old since *old* doesn't' exist yet. (For that matter *yet* didn't exist yet either.) And why should I say it at all? Why am I suddenly thinking of loving?" Spirit would have thought for a long time about that question if he had invented *long* and *time* yet. She thought very hard. Loving, he knew in the *now* of eternity, was very important to her, more important than all the things that he could ever imagine (and she could imagine everything). And so Spirit knew that love was his essence. Love was the energy that drove her boundless imagination. Love was the source of every idea and love was the purpose of every thought. In that instant, in the eternal now of his soaring presence, Spirit knew that her name was Love.

Someday, when days had come to be, philosophers would insist that Spirit was complete in itself, even though its name was Love. They would insist that Love was fulfilled by loving itself, and would even invent strange doctrines saying that Love had a multiple personality, so that the different alter egos of Spirit could love themselves and be complete. Spirit knew that they would play those kinds of mental games because they were already playing them in her imagination. He knew that people would kill one another because of those games. And she knew that those doctrines were more a reflection of the philosophers' narcissism than of her own nature. In his infinite mind Spirit knew that Love was incomplete when there was nothing to love other than oneself and one's ideas.

Love's heart yearned to pour compassion into the hearts of other beings. But she couldn't do it because there was only *being*, only himself. Her heart grew full of longing, full of the wonders of her imagination, and full of an excitement that she would say that she had never known before, if there had been such a thing as *before*. As she soared and played and dipped and dove and rose, the fullness grew and grew until she thought that her heart would explode with her desire to share himself with others. And then it did.

Love watched as all the wonders of her heart streamed into a reality that was outside of her and yet still within her. Quarks showed up first. "Cool," she laughed, rejoicing in their attraction for each other. Hydrogen atoms danced, and then carbon. Flames of primal stars whirled from his heart, and giant black holes, and clusters and galaxies of burning atoms. Love laughed and soared and rejoiced.

Suns formed, and planets, and life began. Love guided them all by the force of his Spirit. Everything came to be by the power of Love, and without Love nothing found its way into existence. Under the guidance of Love, life evolved. Plants grew. Fish swam. Birds flew. Dinosaurs flourished and then were the victims of a divine recall. "I can do better than this," she thought. "My love still needs *more* to be complete."

Love's imagination designed a prototypical being that would love her as she/he already loved it. This being must have a heart as hungry for love as her own, a brain that wanted to understand the complex beauty of all that had poured from her heart, and the freedom to reject him if it chose to—after all, love that is not freely chosen doesn't mean much to the one who receives it. Although Love guided every change in every universe, Love controlled none of them. One possibility in every choice was the one that Love desired for his beloved, but it wasn't the only option. Some universes developed very slowly because of the freedom they had. Love knew that she was risking universal disaster if these new beings used their freedom to reject her, but his outpouring of love meant little if she did not risk giving them that possibility. Of all that she imagined only these beings were like him for only these beings had hearts that craved the fullness of love.

Spirit still soars above creation like a great frigate bird above the waters, and Spirit flows through the whole of creation like a hidden life-giving spring, and everything continues to be guided by the force of Love that holds it all together.

Love delights in everything that exploded from her heart. But Love often struggles with the last being she imagined. Sometimes their brains and their hearts are in terrible conflict with each other. Occasionally one of them discovers some truth and shares it. When that happens, Love's heart soars again with hope.

"You got all that from a frigate bird?"

"You can discover all the secrets that are worth knowing from the smallest atom if you know where to look."

"I like your story," I told the old sailor. "It pulls together quantum physics, evolution, Spirit, God, and creation."

"When you know God," he smiled, "then you know all that is needed. There is no longer a need to argue over whose version of the story is the right one. You are free to write your own story. God is truth. All the *truths* we grasp so tightly are not God although many of them point toward God. People have always mistaken their own truths for God."

"I remember that an old Christian mystic, Meister Eckhart, said 'for the sake of God, you have to give up God.'"

"Yes," continued my partner on the beach. "If you think you know something about God, then you don't know God. What you think you know is an idol that blocks your sight and plugs your ears. There is only one thing that you can say about God: 'God is love.' Everything else is probably wrong. At best it is only a little bit true...."

"Look again at the bird."

It still soared above us, a vision of black and white glory against an azure canvas. I listened now. What the old sailor was telling me challenged things I had once believed, left me a little anxious, and yet sounded a note of harmony in my heart. I was willing to let him chart our course for a little longer.

"Can you capture that bird?"

"No. To capture it, I would have to harm it, perhaps even kill it."

"Listen carefully: you can no more domesticate God than you can make that frigate bird into a pet. A pet god is like a pet rock: it just sits there. Buddha knew the danger of a domestic god. He rejected all talk of God because God is too important to talk about. Nearly everyone's religious language is full of vanity."

This was a little close to home for me. I knew that I was full of doubts and questions, but I didn't want some stranger raising questions about what I wasn't sure that I believed. This was *my* religion, and I wanted to reject it by myself. He had gone to meddling....

He laughed at my frown. "Listen: even Jesus said that you can't capture God in your ideas. He said Spirit is like the wind, and so are those whose lives are renewed by Love's power. They are so unpredictable that you don't know where they're coming from or where they're going. If Jesus and Buddha refused to cage the bird, then what business do you have in doing it? It's OK to reject the god you doubt. The god you reject isn't God anyway. It's just an idol from your past. It's time for you to let it go."

I could feel the burden of belief lift from my shoulders. I had believed in a god that I didn't know, a god that was handed to me by others. Like a shrunken old T-shirt, the god of my childhood made it hard for me to breathe but I kept wearing it anyway. Suddenly I felt the same breeze that carried the bird above me. The wind of Love caressed me.

"Be careful how you think of God," he warned me. "Today's metaphors are tomorrow's idols."

"But I can't think of a divine nothing," I argued.

"You can. God is indeed no-thing. That is the lesson in this for you."

An image came to mind, more a feeling than a vision. I asked the sailor about it. "I am beginning to think of God like the ocean. We are like the fish. We swim in God, but we can't define her, and so we forget that Love surrounds us and is inside us."

He grinned. "That's a good image for now. But hold onto it very loosely. Try to think of God as a Spirit-force that permeates every empty space and every atom of the universe. Your physicists know about the strong and weak forces, about electromagnetic forces, and about gravity. God is the force of Love, present in everything and everyone, that can only be detected by the heart."

I liked what he said. I sailed because it gave me freedom. I liked the idea of a God that is wild and free, a God whose name is Love.

He threw a small rock into the water. "That's a good image for today. Remember to test it again tomorrow, or your free God could turn into a petrified doctrine." The ripples spread out from the splash as we watched.

CHAPTER 6

▼

THE HOLEY MAN

The ripples died slowly as the rock sank. My heart was full of love but my mind was full of questions. "In the story of the frigate bird, you said that there are persons who see the truth and share it. I want to be one of those people."

"You are, but you are not yet."

I didn't get it. "How can I be one of them, and not be one of them at the same time?" His obscurity was beginning to chafe me like the wind chafes a sheet against a shroud.

"Everyone is one of them, and everyone is not yet one of them."

"How can that be?" I asked out of frustration. Like the sailors of old I felt that I was being taken to the edge of the world or at least to the edge of my world, and I might fall off at any moment.

"You don't know yourself," he smiled. "You have no idea who you really are. In the blindness and deafness of your life, you are blind and deaf to your true Self."

I felt angry. I had spent a lot of money on self-help books. I had been to the best therapists I could afford. I had kept journals for thirty years. I had learned to single-hand *Moonghost*, where I could face my inner demons alone, anchored on dark nights at this very island that now was so different from what I had known.

"I've done my inner work," I bristled.

Again he simply smiled. "You've done all of it that you knew how to do. The guides you paid so lavishly couldn't take you where they themselves had not gone. You are far more than you know. Your very being is holy, but you can't learn that until you become holey."

I sensed another story. My anger subsided as my curiosity rose.

"Listen...."

And for a moment there was only the sound of a heron's bark on the beach south of our campfire.

Sam was like any person. He fished, he dove, he read, he studied, he made love, he went to work, he paid his bills, and sometimes, on rare occasions when guilt or yearning forced him, he went to church. Like every man or woman, he had a secret sense that his life fit him too tightly. Like most women or men he didn't talk about that. Appropriate conversation included golf, the stock market, property taxes, football, the decline of public education, and the best investments for retirement. No one discussed or even questioned the way that their lives fit them.

And so Sam wondered whether anyone was like him, really, inside, in his unspoken and unmentionable subtle feeling of constriction. Everyone seemed happy, content, and satisfied. Sam decided he was weird.

He thought. He decided that the thoughts he was thinking were very deep. He lay down in the grass beside his house, looked at the sky through a canopy of oak, and began to wander among the silver wisps of clouds that scudded over his bluegrass pallet.

He played in those clouds. He skipped from cumulus to stratus. A memory condensed in that wonderfully meditative moment. It grew larger and fuller until it rained and soaked him with an awareness that he had always known and always forgotten. A vision of Superman, Batman, Spiderman, Robin Hood, and the Tick filled his eyes.

Sam thought again. "What," he wondered, "could all these people have in common? Why would thoughts of superheroes stop me from seeing these beautiful clouds?" But no answer came. He already knew the answer, but he didn't know it. Revelation is like that: usually obscure and never in neon.

He stood, brushed the grass cuttings from his slacks, and drove to his office to spend the rest of the day in what people mistakenly call "real life." He returned phone calls, wrote memos, and went to a boring and useless meeting. He drove home, drank a glass of red wine ("for my heart," he rationalized), watched some vacuous sitcoms, survived the news by shielding himself from the impact of what the talking heads reported, and tumbled into bed glad to be ending another day that didn't really fit him.

But Sam couldn't fall asleep. He tried to count sheep, but the sheep kept turning into superheroes. When Superman had outpaced a speeding bullet fifty times, the Tick had broken the roofs of forty buildings, and Robin Hood had saved Maid Marian from sixteen evil sheriffs, he bolted from bed and screamed, "Tights! They are all wearing tights!"

So what?

And then Sam had an insight. Although he lived in a world that mistrusted all insights and thought them dangerous, Sam had an authentic realization: "I have been wearing tights all of my life. That's why everything seems so 'tight' to me! I wear tights to school, tights to work, tights to church, and tights to parties. I wear tights in the shower, tights when I swim, and tights when I make love."

He paced his bedroom. It was too tight for his vision. He ran out the back door, fell onto the soft bluegrass, and searched the night sky for the Milky Way. Slowly his mind quieted until he drifted among the stars where he could sift questions and possibilities. He rested on a particularly bright star, just to the left of the crescent moon, and his insight broadened. "Maybe everybody is wearing tights. Maybe that's why no one talks about the truth. Maybe that's why no one mentions the way her lifestyle fits. And maybe that's why love never satisfies."

"Come on," I laughed. "Tights? That's crazy!"

"And you think the earth is flat," replied the old salt. "You think too literally. If you believe that reality can be described in a scientific journal, then you understand neither science nor reality. Your own tights are too small. They're choking your imagination."

"OK." I grumbled. "I'll shut up and loosen up."

The heron barked again. The sailor continued....

Insights and revelations are very personal experiences, but Sam needed to share this one. He told his therapist about it. She told him to hang some crystals in his bathroom to restore his feng shui. He told his golfing buddies about it. They replied that he could correct the hook in his mind by moving his left foot back two inches. Lonely and discouraged, he began to doubt that his "insight" was anything more than mental indigestion. He didn't know, yet, that they couldn't understand him because they were wearing tights.

Tense, worried, uptight, muscles cramped, Sam visited his massage therapist, a New Age woman with wonderful hands. She told him about the harmonic convergence, the rise of Atlantis, the impending reversal of Earth's magnetic field, and the coming movement to reunite the continents. "This woman," he thought, "could listen to anything and not think it's crazy." So he told her about the superheroes, the stars, and the tights. Her gifted hands fed positive *chi* to his spine, her long red hair brushed his back, and she said: "I know a native American shaman who has a sweat lodge in his teepee. When I am confused, I sweat it out. Go to him."

So Sam went. He wasn't sure where he was going. The woman with the wonderful hands was a little vague about directions. All she said was to drive north, head for trees and a lake, and follow his intuition. In Sam's previous lifetime, those kinds of directions were a formula for getting lost but on this day he had no choice. He drove. And he drove. He saw trees. He smelled water. And then, for a reason he didn't understand, he turned left, swept up a hill, curved downward through a stomach-churning dip, swooped past two wide-eyed deer, and headed straight for Red Feather's teepee: a two story, five thousand square foot mansion on the shore of a translucent lake. Red Feather greeted him: "How?"

"What a politically incorrect stereotype!" Sam thought, but replied "How!"

"No," Red Feather laughed. "I mean, how the devil did you find me?"

"I drove until it was time to stop. That's the way I do things these days." Sam had expected a smelly old man in a loincloth, not the lord of a manor dressed in tweed. He began to understand a great truth in life: "Give up expectations. Reality is a lot more interesting."

They shared stories and sipped Cutty Sark on the patio, cooled by the ceiling fan and soothed by the quiet energy of the lake a hundred yards below them. Red Feather, whose *nom de plume* was Ralph Fredricks, told how he had amassed an unexpected but pleasant fortune embedding Native American legends in romance novels. He now lived as a hermit free from the need to indulge the fantasies of lonely liberal ladies and waited for the One to appear. He used his sweat lodge as a lure for the man or woman who would become open to deeper mysteries. Sam, who until his vision in the bluegrass considered himself to be a most ordinary man, shared his insight about the tights, his search for someone who would understand, and his strange path to this place.

Red Feather's pulse quickened as he listened. This was the moment every shaman lived for: he was about to witness the opening of a truly enlightened heart.

"It's time," they both knew. Glasses empty and hearts mellow, they walked a starlit path to Red Feather's sweat lodge, a sauna built on the side of a cliff over the water.

"What about the teepee?" Sam wondered.

"Time to upgrade," Red Feather smiled. "Leave your clothes on this boulder. Leave everything outside this door. Leave your words, your assumptions, and your expectations. Unless you are willing to enter as nothing, you will know nothing."

Suddenly Sam knew that this tweedy author was the shaman who would help him understand his vision. The dry heat burned their feet as they stepped on the cedar floor and singed their buttocks as they sat on the bench. Saying nothing and offering no sign of guidance, Red Feather sprinkled water on the hot rocks, chanted in a language that Sam didn't comprehend, and waited hopefully. Sam began to sweat. Soon he was as wet from head to toe as if he had been standing in a shower. He looked at his companion and saw, for the first time, that the tights were real. They covered Red Feather from head to toe like a full-body unitard that adhered perfectly to each hair of his head, to eyebrows and lids, to nostrils and lips, and to fingers and toes as though they were a second skin. No knowledge explained what Sam was seeing. His knowing was beyond words, a wisdom that filled his awareness as richly as the sweat that pooled at his feet.

"He is the One. My life is complete." Red Feather knew this without knowing how he knew it. His silence grew.

Sam's head tingled. Air moved across his scalp as it had never moved before. His mind grew quiet. A great peace filled his body, every muscle without tension, every anxious thought drifting away. He was ecstatic without movement—beyond emotion, inwardly still. He could not have spoken, for no word forced its way past the silence that was as much a part of him as the lodge's heat.

Sam sat in this peace for a timeless time, and then, slowly, air caressed the hair of his chest, his skin tingled again, and a sense of overwhelming love poured out of his heart. Sam was a funnel of love that poured into his head and out through his chest, filling him as fast as he emptied.

For a time, another time, and a half time, Sam sat and sweated. And then, without a word to his host and mentor, he walked out of the lodge. He left a trail of sweaty footprints and his clothes on the boulder and followed a deer trail to the water. He sat down in a shallow pool to wait.

Sam sat in that pool for fourteen days. Red Feather brought him food and made sure that a fresh towel was nearby. When the time for Sam to begin his new life finally arrived, the two again sipped Cutty on the patio in the breeze of the ceiling fan. But they shared few words. There was no need for either to speak. Sam could not explain what had happened to him. He could not describe the hours he sat in the water. They both knew that Sam was no longer the man that he once had been. He was more deeply himself. Red Feather could feel Sam's love. And Sam knew one truth without doubt: the tights that once bound him, as they bind everyone, had been pierced. A river of Love flowed into the crown of his head and gushed like a spring from his heart.

Late that evening Sam stood in front of a mirror for the first time since he left the sweat lodge. Still naked, he easily saw the tights that covered his own body, as he had seen those of Red Feather. He was surprised that he could see holes in them. The fabric on the crown of his head had melted away. So had the fabric that covered his heart. He laughed: "I came here looking for a holy man. Instead, I've turned into a holey man." And Sam saw more: he saw that his own holey tights were a brilliant soft white in color. Red Feather's had been deep blue. He wondered whether the color of the tights had anything to do with the nature of the person who wore them. "There's a lot," he thought, "that I still have to learn." But he knew this much: for the first time in his life he did not feel unloved and he did not think that he was weird. He knew, somehow, that the weird people were those who were still bound in their tights and did not feel the river of Love. Sam had found himself and something more....

Early the next morning Sam embraced Red Feather (who was nearly knocked unconscious by the power of the love that flowed into his heart,) got into his car and drove. And then he drove some more. And when it seemed to be the right thing to do, he turned to the right and found himself at home. He went to his office, returned phone calls, and sat in useless meetings. He went to parties and listened to talk about retirement plans, real estate investments, and golf. Everything was the same.

And everything was different. When he spoke on the phone, his listeners didn't want him to hang up. There was something in the vibration of his voice that soothed them. When he sat in meetings, he saw people in suits, and he saw the same people in tights. He saw how bound they were and how distant they all were from one another. He felt the fear that drove them to compete with polite viciousness. When he went to parties, he heard the emptiness and longing in their voices. Their talk of golf and investments was like verbal tights that hid their anguish and self-hatred.

Surprising things happened to Sam. Someone at the office cornered him in the men's room and begged for a single touch. This was an extraordinary event. Every man knows that an unspoken social rule forbids all conversation in men's rooms and absolutely outlaws touching. Sam didn't care about social convention any longer. He looked deeply at the man who approached him and saw a few loose threads in the tights around his heart. He touched those threads with his finger. The fabric dissolved. Sam felt the power of love flow through him into the man's heart. When Sam returned to his cubicle, his co-worker followed him.

That evening Sam wanted solitude. He needed to think about what had happened in the men's room. He hid in a darkened booth in the corner shadows of a bar. He watched desperate people perform amazing feats of deception in what is known as Happy Hour. A woman slid into the booth beside him as he brooded. She was a little too blonde, a little too stocky, and a little too old for what she was wearing. Sam didn't notice: all he saw was the loose thread over her heart. Through layers of drippy mascara, her eyes pled for his touch. Sam thought: "Her heart's pretty close to her breasts. If I try to touch her and miss, I'll be in real trouble. But if I don't touch her, I'll leave her alone in her loneliness." There really was no choice: he touched the loose thread above her heart and felt love flow to her as it had flowed to Red Feather and to the stranger in the men's room.

Sam soon learned that some people kept their tights closely bound and well-repaired like suits of spandex armor. Others had loose threads over their hearts as though they unconsciously knew they were imprisoned and had picked and pulled on the fabric in their sleep and during daydreams. Those who were uptight never asked Sam for a touch. In fact, they were often hostile to him. But those whose tights were unraveling saw that he had the power to free their hearts.

He came to familiar people, his friends, his co-workers, and the strangers in the local bar, and most did not accept him. But to those who knew his openness, he gave the power of a loving heart.

The heron barked again. The sky over the lagoon nearly matched the color of the water. I laughed: "Jesus in tights! That sounds like Mel Brooks after Billy Graham worked him over."

"What makes you think it's Jesus?"

"Isn't it obvious? A guy has a baptism experience, though I grant you that Sam's was in sweat, spends some time alone to assimilate it, starts healing people, and finds out that some people don't get it or even oppose him."

"That happens everyday," my companion challenged me. "It can happen to you. That's why I said that most people are and are not yet. Sam was not yet holey, but he was holy."

I was dizzy, the way I get sometimes on a downwind run in fierce waves. My mind was yawing and I wanted some stability. How could this man say that I was anything like Jesus? And how could a silly story about tights have anything to do with the Son of God?

"That's your trouble," he read my thoughts. "You believe the labels but you don't look underneath them."

"O.K.," I agreed, "I know. I'm a hopelessly superficial American who only came out here for a little escape from work. I didn't expect to discuss the human condition and Christological mysteries."

"Good," he laughed. "I don't think you should expect to have your expectations fulfilled. Isn't this more fun?"

"I don't know that it's fun. I think your cargo is getting a little heavy."

"There's more room in your vessel than you know." He laughed again. "If you want to be someone who can see the truth and share it, then you need to understand this: the truth is more serious than you can ever imagine, and the truth is funnier than your prejudice will allow it to be."

"Serious, but not to be taken seriously?" I was trying to follow him. "I'm willing to go all the way with you. Where do we start?"

"With the most outlandish image in the story."

"Tights?"

"You got it! If you don't understand the tights, then you can't understand why Sam became the funnel of love."

I was on a mysterious island with a crusty old salt that came across as a philosopher of the ages, and suddenly I was transported back in time to a dingy old lecture hall in a Gothic granite building. I expected to hear about Descartes and Socrates. But instead he told me about Willie Nelson.

"Do you remember Willie's song 'The Most Unoriginal Sin'? That's where we need to start. The tights are about unoriginal sin. Your theologians have made this idea impossible to understand by misnaming it. They called it 'original sin,' as though someone committed a sin at the human origins."

"You mean it's not all Eve's fault?" I was a little sarcastic.

He stepped up to the challenge. "It's nobody's fault. That's the problem with the word 'sin.' You ought to drop it from the language. There's no one to blame. It's not even a moral issue. It's just the way things are."

"You mean 'sin' doesn't have anything to do with moral behavior?"

"Some does, but not the unoriginal kind. Human beings have been evolving for tens of thousands of years. They've been wearing tights the whole time. It's no one's fault."

I was getting lost again. "Try to make some sense out of this," I begged, "and stop talking in circles. Anyway, I always thought it was about sex."

"It has nothing to do with sex, but it has everything to do with how people do relationships. Think of it this way," he began. "There are two things that all humans fear from birth, and maybe even in the womb: being unloved and being loved. So when a baby slips from its portable spa into the cold world it falls into a pair of invisible tights. It happens so quickly that you would need supraliminal quantum vision to see it."

I was beginning to understand. "The tights are a metaphor for an invisible armor we wear to protect us from fear of love?"

"Yes. They protect us from being loved too deeply, and they protect us from being rejected too severely."

Now I was confused. I knew that we all need defenses to keep from being hurt, but why would we need defenses against being loved?

"Because really being loved requires that we surrender our defenses and feel our oneness with others. Only atom bombs are scarier than that."

I pondered what he said. Maybe, I told myself, we wouldn't need atom bombs if we weren't so afraid of love.

"Yes," he replied to my thoughts. "Power takes the place of love when our lives are ruled by fear. Lovers turn intimate moments into battles for control, and nations turn politics into contests of oppression. When you are wearing tights, real love can be imagined but it can never be experienced. And almost everyone wears tights, including you."

I knew he was right. I knew that there was a part of me that was ambivalent about the very intimacy I wanted with others. I have known that ambivalence since very early in my childhood. Sometimes I felt more comfortable and safer alone. I knew that there was always a subtle barrier between my lover and me even when we made love. And I knew, in my most honest moments, that I didn't really like that barrier even though it gave me a sense of emotional safety.

"That's the loose thread in the tights," he said. "Once they start to unravel, you can't play the old power games any longer. You begin to know that it's all been fake. There must be more."

I thought of my excuses for living within my defenses. I had told myself that wanting "more" in a relationship was a romantic projection of unmet childhood needs or that it was a cultural illusion that interfered with stoical acceptance of reality. But maybe "more" was really just more. I remembered a girl I knew in another lifetime. She was very "loving" towards me but she told me she needed space about the time I began to trust her. I struggled to understand her until an evening we shared at an Italian restaurant. I usually ordered spaghetti and meat sauce, and she usually ordered something she had never tried before. I asked her about that. She said that she liked to taste new things. When I took her home with her doggie bag I looked inside her apartment. Her living room was full of doggie bags, dated and stored alphabetically. She liked new entrees, but she never finished them and never tried the same one twice.... She didn't commit to anything. I knew then that she needed space because of her fear of being loved and that her fear of being loved came from her fear of not being loved. I felt like another doggie bag in her collection of incomplete relationships. So I pulled my own tights a little tighter.

"If we didn't all know there was 'more,' we wouldn't keep trying this crazy dance of relationships?"

"Yes," he answered. "Remember, your heart dances to a different rhythm than your wounded psyche and misinformed mind. Your heart knows that there is a source of love beyond all your fears and defenses."

This was a lot to absorb but there was still more to learn. "I want to be a person who sees the truth and shares it. And I guess, from what I can figure out, that means I want to be more like Jesus."

"And you shall be, as you already are, but you must learn one more thing from the story."

"And what is that?" I didn't understand why the old man couldn't give me a straight answer. I knew that all spiritual masters talked in circles and stories and their disciples spent years afterwards learning the sound of one hand clapping. That sort of riddling didn't appeal to me. I wanted a straight answer, and I was irritated enough to want it *now*!

His laugh was deep and loud. "You want some straight talk? So it shall be. That's the next lesson in all this. Listen! What was Sam able to do after he left Red Feather's lakeside retreat that he couldn't do before?"

"That's easy," I answered. "He could see people without their tights. He could see that their hearts sought love instead of armor."

"Right. Well, if you want to be more like Jesus, since you think that's what this is about, then you have to do the same thing with him."

I objected. "He had no defenses against love. Everybody knows that he is sinless."

He laughed again. I began to think he was playing with me. "Listen carefully with the ears of your heart or else your superficial mind will be offended: you see Jesus in tights too. You don't see him wearing the same defenses that you and all others do, but you see him in an armor that is even more binding."

I always thought of myself as a liberal, open-minded, seeking, honest, tolerant, and forgiving semi-Christian. I had stopped calling myself a Christian many years ago, when the media and the "moral majority" co-opted the term as a synonym for doctrinal intolerance and moral rigidity. But I still loved Jesus, even if I wasn't so sure about all those people who use his name in vain. This crusty old guy had no right to step on my toes!

"I'll pack your feet in ice, if you like, or kiss them, or wash them humbly. Your toes are OK. You might hear something that will set you free if you drop your defensive reactions for a moment."

I shut up and he began to talk. This time the words spoke to my heart.

"You can't see the truth about Jesus because you are wearing religious tights."

"What do you mean?" I asked, this time sincerely. "I have been studying him since I was a child."

"You have spent much energy on those studies. And what do you know about him?"

I proudly answered, "I know that he is the King of Kings, the Lord, Wonderful Counselor, the Messiah, the Christ, the Son of God, born of a Virgin, cousin of John the Baptist, crucified as a criminal, and that he was resurrected from the dead."

He snorted! "Sounds like a doggoned creed to me. This place is holy, but it ain't no church. I asked what *you* know about him, not what a dried-up tradition says. You gave me nothing but formulas."

"But those are the truth," I protested weakly.

"Those are impressions of the truth," he said. "Look, it happened more like this. People who knew him were touched so deeply by the presence of Love that they searched for ways to describe their experience. The labels that you repeated were the best they could do. They hung those labels on Jesus because they needed to have some way of saying that he was special. When they were with him, Love penetrated their defenses and fears. They had a relationship with truth. They were free to love others. That's pretty powerful stuff for people who once lived in tights."

So my "labels" were correct, I thought to myself. But he continued....

"After awhile the people who knew Jesus in the flesh were gone. They left behind their words, the labels and titles you just repeated. But a strange thing happened. As the church grew in power, people grew farther from the experience of Jesus. They didn't know him in the flesh. And those who knew him in the Spirit seemed always to be in conflict with the religious establishment, whose leaders wrote them off as deviants, heretics, and wacko mystics. So the labels that once set people free because they pointed to Love's presence in Jesus became like religious tights."

"I'm confused," I said.

"It's quite simple. Now people use those labels and formulas to avoid looking at Jesus the person. They keep Jesus in a religious cage, with bars made out of doctrines and traditions and labels. All that you know about Jesus are descriptions, not the reality behind them. Your words are defenses against the very thing you say they describe. They protect you from the power of Love that people saw in Jesus. Instead of knowing the power, you pretend to be enlightened by saying the words. If you want to know Jesus, yourself, or anyone else, you've got to get below the words. You've got to know the person."

"So what do I do now?" I was at a loss. I had tried all my life to make sense out of the very thing he was telling me to forget. Sometimes I felt like those old beliefs were all I had.

"You said that you wanted to see and share the truth. That means that you need to examine everything you *thought* was the truth. That's why the story of Sam, the holey man, is so important."

"OK. But how is Jesus like me?" This was the question that haunted me. I knew that if he wasn't like me then he wasn't much good as a savior. But I suspected that if he *was* like me, then he wasn't much of a savior either. It seemed hopeless.

Again the old sailor read my mind. "In the story, Sam was exactly like you, right?"

I agreed.

"And yet he was opened to Love and given insight into others that healed them, right?"

Again I agree.

"Well, start thinking about Jesus the same way. The only difference between you and him was the hole in his defense system. That's what it means to say he was without sin. He let Love flow into him and out of him into the hearts of others who were ready to receive it."

"Are you saying that I can do that, or that anyone on earth can do it?"

"No. I'm saying that you can't *do* it. But I am saying that you can allow it to happen. It's like this: you allow your heart to become an open window to Love. Then when others look through that window, they'll see God."

I thought for a long time. An unusually warm and fresh breeze blew through the lagoon that lifted my spirits and filled me with joy. An open window to Love: that spoke far more clearly to me than a lot of first century formulas that had died a long time ago. And somehow Jesus started to become more real, more human, and more present.

"Sometimes," my wise companion said, "you have to save Jesus from Christianity to know him."

"And always," I added, "you can't know yourself until you know him and look through the window of his heart."

We laughed. It had been a long and complicated tack, but I liked the heading we were on.

CHAPTER 7

▼

REV. BOB'S WINDOW

I took a three-hour walk for a few minutes on the windward side of the island. I usually can see vague outlines of a day mark, a crab trap, some driftwood, or a few wave crests when I'm fogbound. This time I could only look *at* the fog, not into it. It was a solid wall of water vapor.

My sailor friend produced two metal cups and some fresh water. I had no idea where he got them, but by now nothing he did surprised me. He raked some of the fire's orange coals into a depression in the shells. He set the cups on the coals, dropped in a couple of teabags, then, sitting on his haunches, he waited with a smile. The warm wind had stopped as suddenly as it had started and I was chilled. The tea smelled delicious.

"Spices from a small island in the Pacific," he explained.

"When did you get them?" He had appeared on this atoll with no pack, no boat, and nothing in his pockets. My curiosity pushed me to find some way to understand what this guy was about.

"While you were thinking," he offered, "I made a quick voyage."

"Yeah, right! And I had a vision of the Virgin Mary in the fog. Maybe I'll sell tickets to see it, and then I can get a bigger boat and sail to an even stranger island." Again I doubted what he said.

He challenged my cynicism. "You don't believe because you are trapped in a Newtonian mind. You claim to be spiritual but you still believe that what you see and touch are all there is. Loosen up! Time and space are relative. I thought you believed in eternity! It was an easy trip, a long voyage that took no time at all."

Wherever it came from, the tea was just what I needed: warm, gentle, tastefully stimulating, and somehow thought provoking. I needed to be alone to figure some things out. I walked again to the other side of the reef and stared at the fog. Its blankness helped open my mind.

Thoughts assailed my solitude. Could it be that Jesus and I are really no different below the surface? I had always believed that Jesus was fully human. That's what the creed says and I just accepted it. But I knew the creed also said that he was "fully God." How can he be like me if he is fully God?

I began to think the unthinkable. Maybe I am "fully God" too. Maybe God is not a separate substance that was injected into Jesus at his conception or at his baptism. Maybe God is present in all of us as deeply as God was in Jesus. I remembered Paul's sermon in Acts, when he said that we live and move and have our being in God. How could God be separate if we all have our being in him/her? My mind began to dance with the possibility: Jesus and I are one! Jesus and everyone are one! Even Jesus and the child molesters and serial killers are one!

But that's a horrible thought.

"No," my Island Mystic said. I heard his quiet voice though he stood a hundred yards across the sand and shell. "That's not a horrible thought. That's a loving truth. If you look at Jesus, you see yourself. You see your Self, your soul, your true being. There is no separate God-substance that Jesus had and you don't. The difference between him and you is awareness. Unlike you, he knew who he was. When you discover who you are and let go of all your fears, then you'll know. You'll be more and more like him. And then you'll be more and more like your Self."

"But he is the Son of God," I argued, shouting across the beach.

"Yep!" He grinned. I could feel his eyes piercing my "tights" through the distance. "And so are you! So am I! You have all been making a terrible mistake. Jesus' job wasn't to show how he's different from you. His job was to show how you are all alike. He even said that."

This challenged my beliefs but something about it liberated my heart and mind. I still wasn't finished questioning. "But I've always thought of Jesus as the great exception, a one-time act of God."

"That's because you turned him into a religion, and people like to base religions upon exceptions, not on ordinary things. Jesus was an ordinary man with an extra-ordinary awareness of his identity. So were your other heroes, like Socrates, Buddha, and Emerson. But God wasn't doing anything more with them than God wants to do with you or than God did with Sam in the story. There isn't any special God-substance that Jesus had and you don't. *There is only God.*"

With that, my friend looked away. I felt his presence and his distance, and I knew that he wanted me to sit for a while. I sipped the warm tea in the damp air. I had a lot to digest.

My thoughts heated up as the tea grew cold in the cup. All this talk of Jesus made me think of church. I never liked churches very much, but I figured they were necessary evils. I had finally become conscious enough to see the superficiality of our culture and the way that corporations try to control our minds and our desires. I figured that churches were a useful counter to inject a little "God" into the commercial wasteland of television and malls.

Now he stood by my side. I hadn't noticed his approach. "No," he said. "The churches reflect their culture. They talk about a god, but often the god they praise is one created in their own image: shallow, judgmental, obsessed with money, and addicted to power and image and violence."

He was relentless in attacking beliefs I thought I had surrendered a long time ago. They were more a part of me than I realized. "I guess," I replied, "that all this talk of Jesus made me think of church."

"It's time for you to learn how to separate Jesus from religion," he countered.

"How? I don't understand."

"Think of it this way. Religion is about lower consciousness, power, control, and the fear of displeasing God. Its focus is always the past. Jesus is about love, compassion, a life without defensive fear, and openness to the future."

"So Jesus is a threat to religion?"

He laughed. "Jesus had an extreme spiritual awareness. Anyone whose awareness grows is a threat to those who live in the past and think like dinosaurs. It happens all the time."

I could feel another story coming. We walked to the driftwood fire. A gull laughed as I sat on a log, waiting....

Rev. Bob was a simple man who loved the uncomplicated life of Beulahland, deep in East Texas. His heart was as true and straight as the interstate that carved the village into slices of poverty and wealth. "Other" people lived on the "other" side of the highway. Rev. Bob was grateful that the Good Lord had called him to minister on the *right* side, where God's people lived: blessed, straight, traditional, and reliable people, all members of the Pentecostal Full Gospel Premillennialist Temple.

The pines grow thick in this part of east Texas, a region so isolated it was like a nation unto itself. The Reverend liked it that way. Its trees, a natural resource mined by paper companies, looked like money to his congregation. Outsiders rarely stopped in Beulahland. The town didn't want their murders, sexual perversions, and secular humanist values.

Beulahland's leading citizens were all related to the Vines family. A traveler on the interstate could look to the hilltop at the symbol of their goodness crowning the town cemetery. Private pilots often used the Vines' monument as a navigation aid, so tall it stood above the others. With egos as tall as their monument, the Vines believed that Jesus was talking about them when he said, "I am the vine, you are the branches." In Beulahland, the Vines spoke for God, and Rev. Bob spoke for the Vines.

But Rev. Bob was running out of things to say. He couldn't pull a bucket full of inspiration out of a dry well. The Vines were preoccupied with their investments and rarely visited him anymore with sermon suggestions: after all, they knew that religion was a hobby but money was real, and money was getting harder to hoard. Tree-hugging enviro-wackos were recycling so much newsprint that there was little incentive to whack down virgin pine forests. Just last spring the Vines had to postpone replacing the strobe light atop their cemetery marker. And as the Vines dried up, so did Rev. Bob's gospel of prosperity: "God rewards the good. If a family has wealth, it is because God has chosen them for their virtue." Lately God seemed to choose tree huggers more than tree whackers. The Vines passed their hours pondering the obscurity of the sins that caused God to abandon them. Rev. Bob passed his wondering what to preach.

Some preachers pray when the well is shallow. Rev. Bob didn't do that very well, probably because he didn't know the difference between God and the Vines' nephew who signed his check. He sat alone in the sanctuary of the Pentecostal Full Gospel Premillennialist Temple, stared at the window above the baptismal pool, and waited for inspiration. A bronze plaque dedicated the pool to the memory of Thelma Vines. (Thelma drowned during the Rev. Bob's sacramental ministrations last year.) The pool was a wonderful vehicle for heavenly passage, large enough for Olympic competition, equipped with a diving board carved from the cedars of Lebanon, and filled with a hundred thousand gallons of water from the Jordan River; indeed, the crops in Israel failed for lack of irrigation the year the pool was filled. The Reverend thought as deeply as he could about the window above the pool and realized as though seeing truth for the first time that it was completely covered by a tangled web of ivy.

Rev. Bob's hands trembled as he walked to his lushly paneled study, whose wall wore a portrait of Sebastian Vines, the founder of Beulahland. Sent on a mission by forces beyond his ken, he seized scissors from his desk drawer, threw the heavy oak doors of the sanctuary against the building's granite walls (the doors were crafted by Thaddeus Vines and bore a memorial plaque to his honor), and stomped outside. Bob didn't know that he had set his face towards his own Jerusalem.

Each of the building's granite blocks, carried by mule train from the Texas Hill Country, was wrapped in an ivy noose. Like a boa constrictor, the vine's tentacles squeezed life from the stones. Rev. Bob could hear his church, spiritless and gasping for breath, cry out for fresh air.... He plastered his body against the window. His hands tore the spaghetti bowl of branches and his scissors flew like a machete. He stripped away the jungle that had blinded his vision until the hexagonal glass was free for the first time in his captive ministry. Rev Bob finally realized that vines had strangled his entire church—and his own soul.

New life surged through Bob's body when he returned to the pew where a few minutes before he had sat dry and uninspired. His lungs danced with deep breaths. His nostrils flared at the chlorine fumes wafting from the baptismal pool. His ears played with the songs of birds: notes that penetrated the doorway where once the shattered Thaddeus Vines Memorial Doors had shielded silence from nature's harmonies.

But it was not his ears, lungs, or nose that held Bob's attention. It was his eyes. A beatific vision penetrated his soul. The window, once closed and dark, had become a porthole into paradise. Bob was a visitor in the Garden of Eden itself, a spectator in reality more virtual than tangible. He saw Adam and Eve where vines had once obscured the bright light of the Son, naked but not ashamed and walking with God in the cool of the evening. This primal vision's power seared his neurons and softened his heart. Bob would never again be the mouthpiece of the Vines and their gospel of prosperity. But he didn't know that visions are always risky, especially when they come to the professionally religious.

The Reverend blinked, looked again, and saw the naked form of Jesus on the cross. Seven words resounded silently in Bob's mind. The figure twisted in pain. His chest heaved for air with the suffocation of crucifixion while Bob's heaved with the ecstasy of insight. Then Jesus was gone, lifted into heaven, leaving an empty cross.

The Reverend blinked again and saw only birds in the live oaks and Spanish moss draping their branches. Suction marks pocked the glass where once the vines had blinded the worshippers. Everything except the inside of Bob was the way it always was. Some say that trauma is any experience that transcends the ability of our consciousness to comprehend it. This was a traumatic moment for the newly liberated preacher. He stared for hours at the window's new transparency and waited for another revelation but he saw only dust and leaves. He had yet to learn that visions don't have reruns.

The next Sunday morning Bob did not preach the gospel of prosperity. Instead he climbed solemnly into his pulpit, where he stood six feet above contradiction, and told of his vision. He testified to the freedom of release from the vines while several people of that name squirmed in the pews. He witnessed to the splendor of Paradise and its fulfillment on Golgotha. And he did his very best to interpret the meaning of what he saw. But he didn't have the consciousness or the mental tools to make any sense of it. The vision stood on its own while Bob tripped and fell.

Bob's version of his revelation went something like this: God created us to be innocent and childlike, and in our innocence we are naked and not ashamed; God was with Jesus, naked on the cross; and so, if we are to fulfill God's purpose, we must also be naked. He closed with a powerful charge to his flock: the church would now be known as the Full Gospel Pentecostal Assembly Premillennial Temple (Clothing Optional). When the good Reverend tore open a curtain that covered the window the Vines ran from the building in disgust. There, painted in simulated stained glass, was a naked Jesus hovering in golden light above a cross, while Adam and Eve embraced below in ecstatic joy. And then, accompanied by a blast of triumphant trumpets from Miss Susie's electric organ, Bob rent his pulpit robe and stood in all his faux innocence like Adam and Eve at the foot of the cross.

From that day forth Bob preached his gospel of redemption: get naked and get loved by God! He bellowed that good news on loudspeakers across all Beulahland while those predestined to damnation plugged their ears and turned away. Rev. Bob was left with a remnant, those faithful few who were both called and chosen, sitting naked in their pews. The building and its dwellers were stripped of the vines/Vines that had choked their lives. This was surely a victory of faith.

Bob and his followers knew that the truly faithful are persecuted. They rejoiced that their martyrdom came swiftly and effectively. God's machete cut to the quick of the budget of the Full Gospel Premillennial Pentecostal Assembly Temple (Clothing Optional). Each Sunday the faithful left their clothes on a hook by the open door and walked, as in the Garden of Eden, to their appointed pews. But they left less and less in the offering plate. Bob's flock wasn't tightfisted. They simply couldn't give more than they had. The hypocrisy of the rich is often revealed in church conflicts: those with money are the least open to change and the first to leave. Rev. Bob was soon penniless.

One afternoon, deep in prayer beside his open window, breeze from the distant Gulf flowing over his naked body, Bob asked for a sign. God had led him to this point: surely God would empower him to continue his quest. Bob lifted his eyes from his navel to see an eighteen-wheeler flying north on the interstate. Written on the side, in letters that had a holy glow, was: "Ferris Drilling Company—Our Holes are Your Hope." Surely that truck carried the solution to his plight. Bob prayed. Bob meditated. Soon his intuitive powers formed the answer to his prayer. "Ferris" combined with a truck with so many wheels surely spoke of "Ferris Wheels." And Ferris Wheels spoke of a carnival. This was a divine sign. The Full Gospel Premillennial Pentecostal Temple (Clothing Optional) was to host a "Carnival for Christ!"

Bob had attended school only long enough to learn to read. He was afraid that a seminary education might rape his virginal faith in an attack of systematic theology. Once God had provided the Vines to support his ministry. He figured that God would provide equally well for his new path. But Bob didn't know enough about words. He didn't know that "carnival" comes from "carne," and that "carne" means "meat or flesh," and he didn't know that a carnival can be a fleshly event indeed. He wasn't an intellectual giant. He simply wanted to raise funds for his flaccid congregation. His faithful remnant, every bit his equals in sophistication, believed his plan was inspired. They mortgaged their homes to erect a neon sign on the roof of the Temple (Clothing Optional) advertising Beulahland's first "Carnival for Christ."

Late that night a flight from Rio, full of dejected and forlorn revelers, landed in New Orleans for a fuel stop, then flew over Beulahland bound for Chicago. Civic leaders in New Orleans were determined to clean up Bourbon Street. Their PAC, New Orleans Prudes for Excellence (NOPE) had clamped a lid on Mardi Gras. And worse, twenty-three inches of rain had washed out Rio's Carnival. The revelers mourned the traditional pre-Lenten debauchery, the drunken parades, and beads traded for flashes of breast. The travelers had no way to drive out their purities before Lent descended with all of its guilt and shame. What good could Lent offer if they had nothing to feel remorseful about?

But suddenly the jet filled with joyful shouts of Portuguese and Cajun passengers whose eyes beheld their salvation. The pilot struggled to keep his plane level while hopeful revelers pressed against the starboard windows. Below, like a lighthouse in the darkness, flashed their saving words: "Carnival for Christ." Surely this was a progressive step in spiritual growth unimagined by the crusty curmudgeons of the Vatican and NOPE.

The carnival opened that weekend. Billy Joe Taliaferro's country band blasted music from a bandstand strung with colored lights. Tents housed pie-eating contests and beanbag tosses. The main attraction was a big Christian Ferris Wheel on the church's parking lot. A lighted cross was strapped to its struts. A ride on that wheel was like a flight into heaven itself followed by a plunge into the chtonic pits of hell.

The townspeople came. The Vines stayed away-although their curiosity compelled them to drive very slowly past the church on their way to more acceptable destinations. They saw pie-divers covered with pumpkin and cherry and blueberry. They watched children toss beanbags at antique milk bottles and adults reaching for inspiring heights on the cross-covered Ferris Wheel. But mostly they didn't see what was not there: the garments of Rev. Bob's clothing optional congregation. Their prejudiced vision didn't perceive the beauty of Eden restored, and, quite frankly, there was little beauty to behold in the earthly tents of Bob's flock. Since they had no reason to stare any longer, they drove away confirmed in their righteous decision to abandon the church.

God loves ordinary people. God loved the townspeople enough that night to add some spice to their otherwise empty lives. Helicopters spun into Beulahland carrying passengers bound for the holy land they had seen from on high. Spirited pilgrims descended like jet-powered doves to the lawn of the Temple (Clothing Optional). Revelers poured forth like desert-locked Hebrews at the gate of the Promised Land. They were saved. Someone finally understood the whole package: if Lent was to be a sacrifice for Christ, then surely there should be an equally potent Carnival for Christ.

Soon conga lines formed and the little church rang with strange tongues, mostly Cajun and Portuguese. Billy Joe Taliaferro's band played "Walking the Floor over You for Jesus," with apologies to Ernest Tubb. Shocked townspeople, who had stretched the limits of tolerance to accept the *alfresco* non-garb of church members, sheltered their children's eyes from the bare breasts and swaying loins of those who knew how to have a real carnival. There was refuge in East Texas when it rained in Rio! Women clad only in feathers caught beanbags between their legs. Cajuns replaced pies with *beignets.* And couples united the northern and southern hemispheres when their chariots topped the holy wheel and praised the Lord with ecstatic cries as they descended.

The Vines were curious about the helicopters. They drove their BMW's and Cadillacs around the block one more time. The clothing optional temple had gone too far: clothes were no longer merely optional but apparently banned altogether! In unaccustomed family unity each Vine called the sheriff on a cell phone. Their synchronicity produced a busy signal rather than a dispatcher. Again and again they dialed in perfect unity only to find the same busy signal. Sometimes the self-righteous defeat themselves through their zeal.

A quiet man clad in denim walked from the bus station towards the Temple (Clothing Optional). He had come to Beulahland because it was there, and because he was there, and because it was the only place in the universe that night. His dark beard was flecked with gray. A ponytail hung past his collar. His receptive and loving soft eyes were hard that night. They reflected the impenetrable secrets of the heavens. He was handsome and fearful, inviting and frightening. His quiet presence spoke volumes. He had ridden the bus down to Beulahland from Palestine (Texas). His name was Jess.

Jess heard the music. He heard the busy signals at the sheriff's office. He heard the shouts of ecstasy from the holy wheel and Billy Joe's country music. He heard the parents' indignation and the revelers' strangely accented shrieks. He watched as the people of this quiet town adopted the clothing optional heresy of Rev. Bob's liberating vision.

Jess walked into the crowd. He hurled *beignets* into lunar orbit and beanbags through the open window of Bob's study. He wrapped the feather-clad women in shreds of tent. The carnival crowd—shocked, fearful, and disappointed—fell into silence and followed him, less out of devotion than idle curiosity. For them, Jess was another part of a delightful show.

Jess stormed into the sanctuary of the Premillennial Full Gospel Pentecostal Temple (Clothing Optional) swinging a beanbag in his right hand and a stale *beignet* in his left. The crowd, still naked but now a little ashamed, followed. The neon sign on the church's roof brilliantly illuminated the stained glass window of Rev. Bob's vision, pouring its holy light throughout the sanctuary. The nakedness of Jesus, Eve, and Adam danced on the walls and bounced off the pews. Eve's breasts, bountifully represented by the artist, caressed the pulpit.... Jess stopped before the window in apparent reverence. The spellbound crowd held its breath. And then, in a feat of slow-motion ambidextrous perfection, Jess hurled the *beignet* through the heart of the naked Jesus. His right hand flung the beanbag like an ultrasonic fastball between Eve's thighs. Only glass shards drizzling into the baptismal pool broke the moment's silence.

And then the crowd roared with offense and was on Jess like blue crabs on a chicken neck. The wave of humanity, freeing itself of canvas and feathers and holding fast to the orthodoxy of Rev. Bob's vision, forced Jess out the door like a surfer tubed on a North Shore breaker. They tied Jess to the Christian Ferris Wheel with linen shredded from their discarded garments. Jess revolved throughout the night, spread upon the lighted cross, while Billy Joe cranked up his steel guitar's volume.

Carnies struck the remnants of tents in subtle pre-dawn light, loaded the Ferris Wheel on an flatbed semi, and escaped to a place unknown. They left only a wooden cross strung with darkened lights. Linen rags marked the places where Jess had been tied to the wheel of humanity's illusions. It took three days to clean up the mess, recycle the beer bottles, hide the used condoms, and sweep up the pie crumbs, beans, and powdered sugar. It took three days to remove all the glass from the baptismal and mop the floors of the Temple. When all was as it was before the Carnival, only one task remained: to replace the sacred window of Rev. Bob's vision.

CNN had a slow news day. There were no wars or elections, and all the celebrity trials and presidential inquiries were on recess. But they heard rumors of strange happenings in an East Texas town where good religious people got naked with Cajuns and Brazilians. Beulahland was the lead story at 6:00. Bored people from all over the world watched the report, put down their remote controls, forced their hindquarters off their couches, and made pilgrimage to Beulahland. They drove past the cemetery with the big marker that said "Vines." They drove past the respectable Methodist, Episcopal, Presbyterian, and Nazarene churches. They crossed the tracks, sliding and rattling through potholes to the Premillennial Full Gospel Assembly Temple (Clothing Optional??). They stopped in the parking lot, home of the now infamous Carnival for Christ. They knelt in wonder at the marks left in the asphalt by the Ferris Wheel cross. And they walked into the sanctuary to view the famous window.

The window's landscape changed constantly. Everyone saw what Rev. Bob had seen when he was liberated from the vines: trees, sky, and the stuff of ordinary life; but many saw something more, something they couldn't explain. Some saw the beauty of a man and woman, innocent, joyful, and unashamed in the Garden, and others saw the outline of a man against the sky, wearing raiment of denim and a gray-flecked beard. Scientists investigated the window but found only compressed transparent silicone.

In Beulahland even the skeptics from CNN talked late into the night about Jess and the Christian Ferris Wheel. Huddled around their espresso machines, they pondered hints that there might be more than glass in the window. No one saw exactly what anyone else saw, but everyone agreed there was *something* special about it. On Sunday morning Rev. Bob climbed into his pulpit resplendent in his new robe of black and red. All of the alienated exiles returned to the Premillennial Temple that Sunday. All except the Vines. They became Presbyterians.

"I would like to have been there," I laughed. "At least it wasn't a boring church."

"Not for one night," the old sailor agreed, "but, yes, it was boring for most of its existence. Most are. And that's not for God's lack of trying to jazz things up."

"So what happened? Seriously, what went wrong?"

He replied, His face somber, "The same things that always go wrong. It's an endless cycle, at least until the end." He giggled! "Religion is a dangerous thing. It's supposed to be open to God, but it usually prefers to close itself to anything new. If it's founded on someone else's past experience, that's OK. But it has little room for experience of God in the present."

The church wrapped in Vines was familiar. A few wealthy people opposed to change controlled most of the churches I knew. I remembered hearing an old bishop say to his congregation: "If I preach religious heresy, none of you will object. But if I preach economic heresy, you will try to fire me." I had lost hope long ago that the church as I knew it could bring me closer to God. Its leaders had dinosaur brains: "it's heresy to think of anything that we never thought before."

"Your mistrust is well-placed," my mind-reading friend affirmed. "Don't trust the institution. The first item on the agenda of any institution is its own self-preservation. It's tough for God to get equal time with that one."

"So what's the point?" My cynicism was surfacing. I preferred to spend my Sunday mornings worshipping at the Church of the Open Water with my boat as the only pew.

"It's OK to give up on the church but don't give up on God," he said emphatically. "God speaks even to those in spiritual prison. The Vines held Rev. Bob in spiritual bondage, and God gave him a vision anyway."

"Yeah, some vision!" My tone was derisive. I wasn't very impressed by the clothing optional temple.

"You're as thick-headed as Bob!"

I braced myself for a theology lesson....

"Relax. It's not that complicated. Rev. Bob's vision was straight from God, but Bob's interpretation of it was half-baked and stupid. Bob couldn't help it: you can't understand God more deeply than your consciousness allows. He was, shall we say, a bit ignorant. Look again at the vision....

"God was telling him that he wants to be with his people without any barriers to love. That's what it means to be naked but not ashamed. With no reason to hide anything, with complete openness and vulnerability, Adam and Eve could walk with God and enjoy each other. That's the way it should be.

"And then God was telling him, 'I gave you Jesus as a symbol of my love because you humans erect defenses against love and kill those who try to change things. Even if you strip and humiliate him, he loved you enough to go the cross rather than deny his message.'

"You see, it wasn't about getting naked. It was about being loving and open and free. Bob wasn't ready to understand that. Sometimes it can take years to understand a vision. You have to grow into it. That's what Bob had to do."

I grinned. I thought about the last story, about the tights that symbolized our defenses. It was also about getting emotionally and spiritually naked.

"You've got it," he laughed. "And sometimes that can lead to physical nakedness as well, but I don't think it will lead to a clothing optional church."

Something still nagged at me. Why did Jess have to die?

"He didn't."

"You mean he didn't die?"

"No. I mean he didn't *have* to die. Neither, by the way, did Jesus. There was no divine plan that called for Jesus to be crucified. What kind of God would design all of history to lead to the execution of someone who loved him so deeply? It is not God's nature to kill. In fact, it is impossible for God to kill. But it is the nature of many religious people, who love their tradition more than they love God, to find a way to kill those who are different or who challenge them."

"Like Jess?" I asked.

"Yes. To the revelers, Jess was a challenge to their way of life. To the 'righteous and clean cut' of the town, Jess was a shiftless bum. But remember, not all crucifixion is physical. Those who had power in the church socially and economically crucified Rev. Bob. Although he had to wander in the wilderness (clothing optional) for a while, he eventually found new life. That's how God does it: when you kill, God resurrects."

I was amazed by the clarity of his words. The old sailor thought on the rhumb line while my mind tacked back and forth beset by fickle winds. Concepts that had always seemed complicated became simple in his spiritual navigation. I wondered how he knew these things and how he avoided the traps of conventional thinking.

"It's easy," he assured me. "If you know where you start, then you can plot your course anywhere. Most people on a spiritual path start somewhere they are not and spend a lot of energy just getting to the starting line. They look like racing sailboats milling around before the starting gun."

His confidence seemed patronizing to me. I had to challenge him: "And *where*, do tell, is the spiritual starting line?"

It was impossible to anger the old guy. Emerald sparks flew from his eyes as he laughed: "It's the sure and positive experience that God is Love. Anything that is not Love is not God. That's where you start. If you're going to plot a course to enlightenment, you darn well better know where you are when you begin! Most of the journey is in fog. You need good navigation skills and a few books written by those who have had the courage to make the voyage. But your course is your own and the starting line is Love."

I remembered Rev. Bob's window. Some people didn't see anything but trees and sky when they looked through it. Others saw the joy and love that God intended for all people, and still others saw the hope and promise of new life. Their eyes saw what they were ready to see.

I understood then that there are some in the church who would find greater consciousness if only there were leaders who could guide them. And I understood that the vision appears for those who have vision. But why, I worried, could some see while others wanted to remain blind? Why were some "saved" or "chosen" while others were content to be lost?

A dolphin splashed the surface and grinned. My heart smiled with her.

CHAPTER 8

▼

THE DESERT OF
HEARTS

I don't know how long I sat on that log. I don't know how many dolphins leapt, gulls cried, or frigate birds soared. I played with the inside of my mind for a time or two. I had a lot of cargo to unpack, and I had a hunch there would be more. None of it was heavy; in fact, it was in-*light*-ening. But it still was a lot to fit into my soul's hold. I had learned that truth is deep within and cannot be defined; that there are many ways to talk about truth and about God; that most of them are valuable; and that none of them are complete. I knew that creation is the explosion of love into an infinite number of universes, an outflow from the heart of God, and that God is a Spirit-force that permeates everything.

Old Hindus talked about the "veil" of illusion that clouds our minds, and the Hebrews had a God who "lifted the veil" for those who were ready to see the truth: they called it "re-veil-ation." They knew that an invisible net covered me and all of my friends—the "tights" of the Island Mystic's story—that kept us from knowing Love completely. For some reason, we love the veil more than we love re-veil-ation. I guess it's like a friend said when her life was changing and others praised her new path: "My old way of life," she said, "may have been hell. But at least I knew the names of the streets. Sometimes I just want to hold onto the past."

I thought about the men and women who find holes in their veils or tights: the ones we call spiritual masters, like the Buddha, Socrates, Mohammad, the Dalai Lama, Thomas Merton, Martin Luther King, Jr., Mother Teresa, John of the Cross, Meister Eckhart, Julian of Norwich, Hildegard of Bingen, and Thich Nhat Hanh. I especially wondered about Jesus. If he is like me, then why am I not more like him? What made him so open and transparent to love? Why are those who claim to follow him often like Rev. Bob's flock, captured by their culture and their limited consciousness?

"There you go again," the sailor knew my thoughts. He sat down beside me. "You're hung up on this 'Jesus' question. Accept that he was a person and that somehow he still *is* a person. Stop trying to explain things that won't fit in your mind. You want to know how to be like him. That's the wrong question."

"Come on!" I feared that his theological rifle was targeting another of my sacred cows. "I thought that I was supposed to be more Christ-like. I won't believe that I am who I should be until I can heal and teach as he did."

"You're dancin' to the wrong tune," he explained. "You think you should *be* Jesus, instead of being *like* him. You can't be him anymore than you can be Sarah Jessica Parker."

I had been confused by the "Jesus question" and "God's will for me" for a long time. I wasn't sure that this guy was going to help any, but I was willing to listen. "Go ahead," I said. "Try to make sense out of it for me. No one else has...."

"It's really very easy. You and Jesus have the same job that Bill Gates and Julia Roberts have. Everyone does."

"And what is that?" I was taunting him, frustrated.

"You are to become God-barers to everyone you meet."

"Right!" I wanted to hit him. He wasn't making any sense. "How can I bear God to anyone? I'm a world champion sinner. I'm not very religious, and I'm *not* like Jesus."

"You don't get it. You aren't to *bear* God anywhere. You can't. You can't possibly take God anyplace new, because God has already been there from the beginning. But you can *bare* God to others. You can show them the Lover who has been waiting for them all of their lives."

He was on the rhumb line again while I was sailing forty degrees off course. What he said made simple sense.

"Look. Jesus was like Sam: he opened holes in all his defenses so that Love could flow through him to others. And Jesus was like Rev. Bob's window: when people looked through him, if they had the eyes to see, they could see God. That's your job and everyone's job: to uncover the presence of God, to bare God, by being transparent to Love's presence in your own life."

I still wondered how I could be more like Jesus.

"Wrong question. If you were supposed to be like Jesus, then God would have reincarnated Jesus in your body. Your abilities are not the same as his but yours are needed in this universe just as much as his were. Stop trying to be like him and start being like *yourself*. That's the only way you can bare God to others."

There was a time in my life when I thought I knew how to be myself, but these days I wasn't so sure. I conformed to others more than I wanted. I was the product of my dysfunctional childhood more than I cared to be. I tried to please people at the expense of my own truth. I talked about simplicity but was a compulsive consumer. I wanted to be authentic but I felt like a fake.

"Sometimes you need another person," he assured me. "Sometimes a *soul friend* can open your heart and show you the way. Even great masters get confused or lost on their voyages. When it's too cloudy to take a sun-shot, your GPS is broken, and your dead-reckoning has died, you need some help from a friend to get wind in your sails again."

Another story was coming. I needed it....

Once upon a time a faithful disciple was burned out. The disciple had tried all of his life to understand what Spirit required of him but as he neared the end of his journey he knew less than he did at the beginning.

His zeal was tuckered and torn. He was an alien in his own body, broken, discouraged, and depressed. He'd failed to find answers. Now he wasn't sure he'd even asked the right questions. And so he gave up. He collapsed on the shoulder of life's road, wrapped himself in a body shrunken into emptiness, and enfolded himself in skin like a cracked, dry, leather wineskin. Breath moved slowly in dusty lungs while he waited for the friendly enemy of death to save him from his torment.

A pilgrim happened upon his improvised deathbed, her step full of bounce and a joyful song on her lips. She slowed when she saw the old disciple on the roadside. He recognized her: they had been students together. "Why," he wondered, "is this woman younger than when we first met, dancing on life's roadway, while I am old, withered, and courting death?"

She knelt beside the old man. Her long red hair tenderly caressed his cheeks. Her tear-filled eyes beamed compassion into his vacant pupils. A spark of recognition flickered within her heart for she knew that this weathered and folded flesh was once her companion. She carefully, lovingly, and gently pulled a canteen from her pack. It was wrapped in canvas as worn as his skin but it was cool to her fingers. It was easy in her hand though it was large and full. She twisted the cork that sealed it and unleashed a shaft of emerald light from its depths. She touched the old man's face, smiled sweetly into his eyes, and tilted the canteen until water streamed over his forehead and ran into his ears and down his chin on its way to the barren soil. The water danced with life when he drank, splashed playfully into his body and rebirthed wonder in his gloomy mind.

Like a skeleton in Ezekiel's valley of dry bones, he slowly knit sinews and unraveled time. Living water saturated his folded skin and stretched youthful tautness over firm muscles. He was as fresh as the day he had started his journey.

His name was John. He was an ordinary seeker in an ordinary world. He assumed that Kathryn, his ageless companion, was the same. But something about Kathryn mystified him as though she possessed a truth that he had not experienced. "Where did you find this water?" he asked.

"Simple," she replied. "It's just over that hill through the desert wilderness."

"How will I know when I am in the wilderness?" John had no clue where he was going.

Her answer was enigmatic: "The wilderness is called the Desert of Hearts. There are no maps. You can easily get lost. But you will find your way to the Living Water."

John felt a flash of irritation. Why wouldn't Kathryn give him a straight answer? "These spiritual types are all the same: they like to be mysterious and confusing. Sometimes I'm fed up with their games!"

She knew his thoughts. "It's not a game. I can't tell you more than that. To know more than that, you need to look for yourself."

John had to accept her words. He had tried everything else and was still empty. She had something he desperately wanted. His body still pulsed with the power of the strange water that she gave him. So John left the familiar road, the pathway that everyone else traveled on their journeys, and struck off towards the hill to look for the Desert of Hearts.

It was a miserable trip as spiritual trials go. The heat index must have been 120 degrees. Rocks cut his toes, and thorns tore his flesh and clothes. Sun blistered his brow. Mountain lions roared in the brush, snakes scampered beneath his feet, and coyotes stalked every step. Even though he could be eaten by a wild beast or poisoned by a serpent he was strangely confident. After all, he had been near death. He had nothing to lose in this wilderness. The Living Water continued to refresh his body and buoy his mind. As long as it coursed through him nothing negative could overwhelm him.

John stumbled into his first oasis. Something about it was familiar. In the distance he saw the oak trees he had climbed as a child. He laughed at a gnarled branch as he remembered when he had fallen, broken his arm, and had the good luck to be unable to perform at a dance recital. He looked nostalgically at the old house, its spreading veranda and red brick, the flagpole in the front yard: this was once his home if ever he had felt at home anywhere. He climbed the porch's steps and peeked through a window. The old chairs he used to push together to make a train were still in the living room. Across the room and through a pocket-door he saw his childhood family gathered around a large mahogany table. But they didn't behave the way he remembered them. It was as though the inside of their souls showed on the outside. Mountains of food towered to the ceiling yet every person at the table stuffed open gullets as though they were starved. They consumed but were never satisfied. Food flowed from their chins to the floor, and still they ate. If the children refused to eat for even a moment, an adult threatened them with beating or isolation. This family allowed no independent thought or motive. Their fear of emptiness determined their interaction.

Except for one young man that John didn't recognize. Quiet, bearded, and dressed in jeans and an unsoiled white shirt, he did not eat but smiled contentedly while others frantically filled their infinite emptiness. Only he detected John's presence. Puzzled, John asked why he didn't consume mass quantities as the others did. The young man answered: "You have enough. I am enough for you."

And then the oasis was gone like the fog of a dream stolen by an alarm. John trudged through the rocky heat of the Desert of Hearts along a trail that was clear to him yet unmarked and never before traveled, and he pondered what he had seen. There was something about his family's bizarre behavior that looked normal to him: he realized that many people in his life consumed as though there was a hidden abyss within them. He was more a part of that family than he wanted to admit. He had consumed others in his hunger for relationship, always in fear of being deprived or abandoned. He had never known what the young man felt: that he had enough. He did not understand the man's words: "I am enough for you."

It looked like a mirage on the horizon. Dragging himself towards a green palm-lined lawn, John saw that this oasis had only one building, a cathedral of granite with massive flying buttresses and gargoyles warding off demons. When he walked to his right, the stones gave way to metal siding, a cheap metal roof, and a mail-order steeple. Experimenting, he walked to his left, where the stones became the simple brick of a storefront soup kitchen. This was the oasis of the Church of All Religion, marked with crescent moon and cross, with statues of Mary and of Buddha, with the Star of David, and with the turbans of the Sikhs. He smiled to himself, relieved: "I have found it! Surely there is a well here where people draw Living Water to fill their canteens and their hearts." Loudspeakers called Muslims to prayer, Baptists to the altar, Catholics to mass, Jews to the Sabbath, and Buddhists to sit. People swirled and genuflected and chanted. But John's happiness soon faded, for each worshipper ignored the others. Christians acted as though Buddhists were invisible, Catholics shunned Protestants, Jews turned their backs on Hindus, and Muslims closed their eyes as they knelt on their prayer rugs. "They act superior to one another," he mused. "Can't they see their unity?"

In the center of the building was a well. Each person who went to it pushed away those who believed differently. Each person shoved a bucket down the long shaft, cotton rope slipping through grasping fingers and burning palms, and hoped to draw Living Water. Each person eagerly retrieved his or her bucket and shielded it from infidels. Every bucket sloshed water as it left the well, but every believer's load turned to sand before it could be tasted. John's countenance fell. "It's not here either."

A young man in an unsoiled white shirt stood in the shade of a date palm drinking water from his bucket. "There is more than enough water for all," he told John, "but only if they share what comes from the well. Because they fear the other's water is poison, their own turns to sand. They use words that can quench their thirst yet they remain dry."

"What about you," John asked. "Why can you drink while they do not?"

"You have enough," he answered. "I am enough for you."

John didn't understand. He didn't know this young man, and he did not understand his outlandish claim. And so he turned his back, afraid that more conversation would distract him from the search for the source of Living Water.

He walked intensely and vigorously and soon approached a third oasis ringed with cherry trees in full bloom. Peering through the branches he saw the monuments and halls of justice he had studied as a child. To the left of the capitol dome stood the Kremlin and to its right were the mosques of Baghdad next door to the Knesset and the Assembly of the United Nations. John walked with reverent awe toward these icons of political power now clustered in one place. But his hope crashed when he heard angry threats of war rather than the gavel of orderly and respectful debate. Half the leaders of the world were tied to trees, and the other half shouted in their faces: "If you could see the truth, and if you would recognize that I control the truth, then there would be peace. There can be peace only if you accept my way. Yours is the way of war." After that tirade, the leaders were released from the trees, the formerly free politicians were then bound, and the same words were repeated. John listened for what seemed hundreds of years as words of hate, war and domination were launched like verbal missiles. Never was there peace. Nothing changed.

John found no Living Water in the halls of justice. Discouraged, thirsty, and tired, he trudged back to the Desert of Hearts. He passed the Lincoln Memorial and headed for the sand and rocks. A young man in an unsoiled white shirt sat in Abe's chair, and John heard these words, "They fight for control because they think they don't have enough. You have enough. I am enough for you."

Would he never find the source of Living Water? John was beginning to think that this Desert of Hearts was a deception without heart, a boundless land filled with oases of illusion. And always, those strange words. Who was that quiet young man?

"These visions, these oases, must be hallucinations," John thought. "The heat's getting to me." But he couldn't shake the feeling that there was another reality, another realm or dimension, where peace is possible, where spiritual unity prevails, and where all hungers are satisfied. He wondered if this strange young man, who appeared in every oasis and every dreamlike vision, knew anything about this other reality. "I must find him again," John's need was suddenly urgent. "He's the only hope in this Desert of Hearts."

As though on cue, a fourth oasis loomed in the sand and rocks. By this time John wasn't surprised to see it spring up in the desert. Gone were the mountainous piles of food, the religious arrogance, and the warring politicians. This oasis was an amusement park built on a scale not even Disney could have imagined. Here the rides ranged from "death defying" to "death challenging" and death always won. Men and women parachuted from mountaintops and dove from airplanes. Football players butted heads. Cowboys rode bulls. Women filled their SUVs with screaming toddlers and raced trains across railroad crossings. Gamblers bet their life savings on a roll of the dice, and headbangers dropped crystal meth. Despite all this frantic activity, despite all this corporately programmed "fun," John saw no one smile. The "guests" of the park navigated its venues with vacant eyes and wrinkled brows, anxious that their adrenaline level would drop before they could reach the next attraction. John used to think he was a spoilsport because he didn't like amusement parks. Now he knew that they weren't amusing. At best, they provided a few seconds of diversion in an otherwise deadly life.

John saw what the patrons' blank stares could not see. He found stacks of dead bodies beneath the roller coasters, under the skydivers' planes, around the rodeo arena, in the back rooms of the casinos, and in the parking lots of the dance halls. All had taken risks to escape their ennui. All hoped that by tempting death they might find a moment of life. All were not amused. All had lost and died.

All, except for one serene young man, wearing an unsoiled white shirt. He sat beside the bodies and subtly smiled. Others dared death in frantic activity. This young man was quiet and at peace. Once more John approached him, and once more the man spoke: "I do not risk death because I know how to live. They risk and die because they don't have enough life. You have enough. I am enough for you."

This vision faded as the others had. John's mind struggled to keep up with his racing heart: somehow he knew that there would be no more oases. He had failed his last chance to find the Living Water in the Desert of Hearts. He must find the serene young man in the white shirt if he was to survive in that desert. Only he had a clue about how to live creatively in the chaos that appeared around him.

John didn't have to leave the oasis to re-enter the desert. The vision simply faded and the desert appeared. He blinked his eyes once, and his feet were on the sandy trail that was his alone. He blinked again, and rocks and mesas surrounded him. John meditated on a red sandstone boulder. Something was forming in his mind, moving upward from his gut, through his heart—less an idea than an insight. He had *not* been traveling anywhere. He had *not* walked on sand, or tripped on rocks. He had *not* visited any oases. No one else was on the path he followed because it was within him. John had been traveling that path through his own life. The Desert of *the* Hearts was really the Desert of *his* Heart. The barren ground was the void within his breast. He was the one who consumed material goods and relationships like a ravenous wild beast. He was the one who looked for the "one true" faith and arrogantly condemned those who were different. He was the one who wanted to control those who disagreed with him. He was the one who tried to deny death by driving too fast, diving too deep, or eating Mexican food. He lived in the Desert of his own Heart. Where, now, when he was ready to learn, was the serene young man?

Suddenly the young man was beside him, wearing that same white shirt. He offered John a drink from his canteen: emerald light flowed from its mouth as it did when Kathryn renewed his life. The young man touched his chest and water danced over his body, soaked his hair, and flowed past his lips. In that touch John discovered the destination of his entire life's pilgrimage. The young man's words were true: he had enough. The touch of this man was enough, his love was enough, and for an instant John knew deep contentment. The young man's love filled him, released all desire to use and manipulate others to fill his own emptiness, ended all desire to find truth in cultural religions, overcame all need to force his will on others, and broke death's grasp on his emotions. Even death became a friend because life was within him.

"If the desert was within me," John thought, "then so were the oases. They were all failed programs I used to find happiness without facing the truth. And that means the young man lives within me as well. I knew the source of Living Water all the time and did not know it."

Water makes the desert bloom. Living Water makes the desert of the heart bloom. John stood again on the roadside with Kathryn. He took her hand and they walked with joy through the lush landscape.

"I think I know my way around that desert," I told the old sailor, "but who's Jesus? Was it that young man in the white shirt?"

"Yes and no. You know that there are no straight answers in the spiritual realm, which is the only real realm. Words are only pointers to a deeper reality, and they often are not enough."

"So stop fooling around," I insisted. "I need to know this."

"If you must know, they both are 'types' of Jesus. Only Jesus was Jesus. But there are millions of 'Jesus' types."

"How can they both be the same type of person?" This was beginning to sound like a verbal pretzel, and I needed to straighten it out at least a little.

"The young man was a 'type' of Jesus before he ever met John. As far as the story is concerned, he was that way from the beginning. John started to become that way at the end."

This was getting a little too far out for me. I wondered whether my friend was talking about reincarnation. Maybe he meant that Jesus was reborn into the body of the young man and of John.

"No!" He was adamant this time. "No! That would do violation to both the man and John. If you want to be like Jesus, don't try to become him. That is a horrible desecration of the most holy temple you will ever know—your own heart. That completely defeats the idea that you are a unique creature. There is only one of you, ever! You are a divine gift to this universe. Why should you try to be someone else, or think that you are fulfilled if you become someone else? There's entirely too much of that kind of conformity in your world already."

I was practically begging. "Just *say* it," I pleaded.

The old sailor was far more patient than I. He turned his warm eyes to me: "It's easy to be like Jesus and to keep God's will. I'll explain it in one sentence, and you will spend the rest of your life learning how profoundly simple and difficult it is. I said it before: *be as fully yourself as Jesus was himself.*"

"That's it? That's all there is to it?"

"Yes. It's that easy. That's what John learned in our story—the young man who set him free was part of his own deep Self. But everything in your world struggles against your doing it. To be yourself you have to know yourself, and to know yourself you have to know God. When you know God, then you will know yourself, and you will be a God-barer to others."

More pretzels. The old salt had a barrel full of them.

He grinned. "Stop making it tough. It's a gentle truth. Your real Self is part of God. If you live from that part of your being you will automatically bare God to others. You won't have to think about it; indeed, it's probably better that you just live your life and not *try* to make God evident. When people see you as you truly are, they will be looking at God."

"That's how it was with Jesus. But I think it's arrogant for me to think I can have that same connection with God."

He grinned again. "That's your religious shame talking. You are programmed to think less of yourself than you are. Even the psalmist said that you are just a little less than the angels and Paul called you God's work of art. Isn't the arrogance on your side? What right have you to demean what God has found precious? Jesus came to show you who you truly are—who you could become if you are open to the flow of Love's Spirit. That scares most religious people, but it's a ticket to freedom for you."

Something still troubled me. I could not get rid of the idea that there was a different substance in Jesus than there is in me. How could I possibly think that I could become as he was? I just didn't have the potential. He must be some kind of supernatural genetic freak.

My mentor looked a bit exasperated. His patience was as broad as the sea and as deep as the surrounding mist but I suspected that he was beginning to find my mind a little foggy. We watched the quiet lagoon for a few minutes. I figured he was waiting for his ideas to sink into my memory bank. Suddenly he was on his feet, pointing and shouting: "Look! What do you see?"

A spring of emerald water had bubbled though the shells at my feet. Its flow was gentle. I touched the delightful water. It was warm.

"Look again!" he shouted and pointed to the south end of the island. A spring appeared there as well, erupting like a geyser and freezing as it landed on the shell. "Look over there!" he yelled, pointing to the north end. A spring of steaming water filled a depression in the beach. He motioned for me to follow him.

"Get undressed," he ordered.

"My tights?"

"You catch on quickly." He peeled off his simple clothes and together we settled into the warm emerald water. I felt the flow beneath me like jets in a hot tub. Water danced around me and showered the bank with sparks. It energized me. I felt like John bathing in Living Water.

"That's it!" he cried. "You are *always* bathing in Living Water, but you don't always remember it. Your life gets dry, but it doesn't have to. Sometimes you're like a fish that forgets about the ocean. The water is all around you.

"Look at the spring that was at your feet. What is it like?"

"It's slow, bubbly, and lukewarm, more a trickle than a stream."

"Good. Now look at the south end. What is that spring like?"

"Like a geyser of ice water. It shoots into the air and freezes before it hits the beach."

"And the one we're sitting in?"

I was beginning to get the point. Sometimes my mind is slower than a sloop in a Force One wind. "Warm, soothing, and life-giving," I answered.

"Almost," he said. "They all give some kind of life. Now think: where do they come from?"

I saw now where he was leading me. I knew that they must all come from the same source yet they were all different. Underneath the island is a stream. Its water appears different when it comes to the surface in separate places but it's the same water.

"Yes." He smiled across our natural hot tub. "So it is with the Spirit-force of Love that you call God. In one Self it emerges as a gentle humility, and in another as strong energy, and yet in another as nurturing peace. The Spirit that was in Jesus is also in you. If you want to know your Self, know that Spirit. That's who you really are. If you try to copy someone else's life, you won't ever live your own."

"So at the deepest part of our Selves we're all one?"

"Different, but one. Yes."

We sat for a while but my questions denied the warm water's peace. "What about the woman in the story? You said that sometimes we need a soul friend?" I was moved by the role Kathryn played for John. Without her he would have died by the roadside. I often have yearned for a person to play that part in my own life: someone to bring me life when I was ready to quit. They were navigators, people who point the way when I sail in circles.

"She was a great gift to John," he whispered. "Once someone was such a gift to me when I was dying…. She was a soul friend to him. A soul friend is someone who can see through our tights-someone who knows who we really are behind the masks we wear and the defenses we use."

I thought of the friends I had known and the ones who support my life now. I was gifted in ways I did not appreciate with people who accepted my fears and failures and still offered me love. One of those friends had told me to make this foggy voyage knowing that I had had my fill of offices and performance. I knew what a soul friend was: I just didn't have a name for it.

He whispered again: "Give thanks every day for those people who can see the truth of your being. They are rare. They are the ones who are with you on your journey, who nourish you when you are hungry, and who— like Kathryn—know when to leave you alone until you are ready for a deeper level of companionship."

His words opened my consciousness to the many soul friends I had been given. Some were trained spiritual directors, one was a therapist, one was a pastor who had outgrown his ordination, one was a fellow sailor, and one—more a soul mate than friend—was my lover and life partner. We all drank from the same spring and shared the same Living Water, though it flowed at different rates and temperatures in the uniqueness of our lives. We were all one. I had always known a love-hate relationship with religion and churches. I now knew this network of soul friends was my church. I had a personal church that I hadn't recognized because I was looking for a religious stereotype.

We sat quietly. The warm water danced on our skin, soaked into our pores, and penetrated our souls.

CHAPTER 9

▼

LOVE ON A LOG

I stared across the lagoon at *Moonghost*. She waited patiently while I simmered with contentment like a boiled shrimp in our natural hot tub. I could have soaked there for the rest of my life. My skin might resemble a prune but my soul would be smooth and blissful.

"Everything must change, and the most important thing stays the same." The old sailor read my feelings and spouted his witty wisdom again. I didn't want to think about it. I didn't want to think at all. I had done enough thinking that day to justify several years of mindlessness. "Leave me alone," I thought.

"Never. Never shall I leave you alone. Now that you have known me, you will never be without me."

I looked at him as he simmered beside me. His lips hadn't moved. His eyes were closed. I was hearing his voice inside my head. "Now I understand," I thought. "I'm going nuts. This whole afternoon has been a hallucination. It isn't real."

I heard the voice, his voice, again: "This has been the most *real* day of your life. Most of your days are unreal. Most of the time that you think you're sailing you're still moored securely to your pier. Your real voyage started this morning. Everything before this was just practice."

I sat a little straighter and stirred the water with my left hand. "OK," I said, "now that you've taken up residence in my mind"—

"I didn't. I've always been there."

"Now that I know that you're there, what do you mean: everything must change, and the most important thing stays the same? Seems like you've dipped into the pretzel barrel again."

He chuckled! "Actually, you know what I mean. Think for a moment: what stays the same always?"

This one I knew, finally. It was the basic truth I had come to this strange island to learn: "The Spirit-force of Love that permeates everything."

"Yes. And what must change?"

This one was obvious: "Everything else."

He smiled. "Heraclites was right. You can't sit in the same hot tub twice."

I wondered what that had to do with anything.

"It's almost time for you to leave this island. When you leave, it will leave as well. I will be gone, and I will always be with you. Though you are contented now, too much contentment will make you as stagnant as this water will be tomorrow. Your voyage needs a few storms, an occasional rogue wave, and some doldrums if it is to be real. If you anchor for too long in one spot, your keel will grow to the bottom and you will die while you live."

I knew his words were true. I didn't like being becalmed: slatting sails and lack of direction drove me crazy. I needed to keep moving. I would soon leave this island and the old salt's peaceful presence.

"You will leave, but you will never leave." The water mirrored his grin.

"I get it. But my body and my boat need to set sail."

"Yes. I have one very small bit of cargo to add to your mind's hold. Do you have room for it, or should I save it for our next morning together?"

My heart leapt! "You mean this isn't all there is?"

He laughed out loud: "Sometimes your mind is thicker than this fog. Do you think that you can learn all of my secrets and hear all my tales in one day? Your cargo is already larger than you can manage. When the time is right, my dolphin guides will find you. Until then, answer me: can you handle one more story?"

I didn't know whether I could handle more, but I also knew that I couldn't refuse this man's offer. After all, he set the agenda for this meeting. All that I did was show up, and I hadn't intended to do that much. If he had more to offer, I could receive it.

I contemplated the mystery of his eyes then nodded my head. "I'm ready." He began to talk....

Pete's soul shriveled in the cold warmth of the subdivision where he lived. The weather was tropical but the atmosphere in his home was freezing. He had everything—the car, the house, the pool, the trophy wife, the yacht—yet icy emptiness tugged at his chest every morning. Nothing warmed him. He tried meditation, Tai Chi, yoga, Christian fundamentalism (he'd gotten saved at least five times!), and alcohol, but the cold void was still there. Running provided the only relief. Pete wondered if he was running away from something, but he ran anyway.

That morning he pulled on his nylon shorts, laced his $200 shoes, and headed for his favorite trail where water oaks bordered a bayou. Sometimes he saw alligators and deer as he ran along the shore. A light gulf breeze brushed his skin. Puffs of cumulus clouds scudded through a deep blue sky. There was something special about this day. Like lots of people, Pete was a closet mystic—so closeted that he rarely opened the door and looked inside that part of himself. "Maybe," he thought, "I'm not running *away* from something. Maybe I'm running *toward* it."

Instances of ecstasy occasionally invaded Pete's ennui. Wind, clouds, trees, water, and the rhythmic crunch of crushed granite were a symphony for his frozen heart. He marveled as sweat poured into his eyes: "I'm warm!"

He rounded a downhill curve towards the bayou and saw *it* on the rotting trunk of an oak felled by last year's hurricane. *It* sat at the edge of his jogging trail like a stray kitten after a frog-strangling rain. Pete ran to escape the illusory prison of his life or, perhaps, to *find* life. But *it* didn't do anything. *It* did not move. *It* did not "work out." *It* did not work at all. *It* sat...broken.

Pete wondered about the unidentified sitting object. *It* must be a weary mother at rest, head in hands, after watching her children leave in the yellow can that carried them to tax-paid childcare. She must be tired and discouraged, searching for joy's revival in songs of the forest's birds. No....

Pete approached *it* cautiously: perhaps, he hoped, *it* is a girl, skipping school to play and waiting for friends to join her. This he wanted: for *it* to be a fresh and spirited girl renewing her senses between the forest and the water.

Pete's heart stopped as he ran past *it*. *It* was a boy of perhaps fifteen years. Sagged on a rotting log and head bowed in a prayer to despair: *it* looked like no one in particular. Pete knew how that felt. The boy's arms were thin and weak, not pumped with adolescent machismo bulk. His hair was stringy and matted. His clothes, a teen's sign of belonging, betrayed his social exile. No face, no clothes, no hair, and no body: *it* was nobody on a log alone.

Pete's heart ached. The scene behind him was an external tableau of his inner reality. Everything about *it* screamed in lonely pain. The boy was a vessel that no one had filled. He was merely an object, his life a swamp of rejection, ridicule, abandonment, and abuse. He had forged an identity out of his suffering: "I am lost and rejected; therefore, I am." He spurned every approach of potential friends. He repelled the touch of repentant parents. He mocked those who preached religion's hope. If he accepted others, he lost individuality. To be found was to lose himself, for only in being lost to others could he find what little self he knew.

A radio's earphones sat like a vise on *its* scraggy head. They poured the promises of a pop world into this empty container: heavy metal's loud passionless boredom, punctuated by DJs chattering about a party he/*it* would never attend. The music's anesthetic inanity lured *it*/him into pseudo-serenity, aspirin for his psychic pain.

Pete stopped to watch, surprised that he was identifying with this creature from a world unknown to him....

"I love you." *It* lifted *its* head from *its* dangle of shame. Static? Judas Priest or Smashing Pumpkins never said those words. In his world, to his ears, in his entire life, those words were unintelligible, a hiss on life's tape or a scratch on a CD without meaning.

"I love you." The words crashed above the guitars and bass. Those words had always flowed like mercury around the barriers of his soul when someone spoke them. Now, like cotton hammers, they pounded him in stereo. Their relentless assault pulsed to the drum's beat and soared with the guitars' solos. He could not tolerate their intrusion. Again and again and again they rang in his ears until they became one Word: "I love you I love you I love you I love you I love you I love you...."

Pete knew. He did not know how he knew, but he could sense the boy's battle. It was the same one that ensured the void in his heart. He and the boy were one.

"NO! Love will destroy me," the youth's roar shattered the wooded silence. "I can't be loved. I can be rejected. I can be hated. I can be teased and taunted. But I can't be loved. That is *not* who I am! Please, NO!" But the pounding beat of the multi-worded Word played on. Unable to assimilate another sound, the boy rose to life. He hurled the headset deep into the bayou and raised his eyes to search the heavens for freedom from his destroyer. When Satan is all one knows, then God becomes a Satan.... He yearned for silence. Even silence—as terrifying as it had always been— promised a wretched safety more tolerable than the agapaic protestations of his divine accuser.

The beat rocked on: "I love you I love you I love you...." Now Pete could hear it echoing through his skull as it penetrated his inner armor. The boy ran deeper into the forest. He vainly tried to flee the Word's words on seldom-used muscles, but his futile flight led nowhere. He stopped, hoping that he was free of the Word's torment so that he could return to his familiar self-contempt, only to hear—no, feel—the words again. His agonized screams reflected his deconstruction. He could not escape the awe-full thing that stalked him.

Pete waited behind a tree. The boy's struggle had been his own for more years than he could remember. Pete was ready to surrender his armor and the useless mask of his false identity. He was ready to offer up the daily pain of an empty heart that nothing on earth could fill. He hoped—perhaps he even prayed, though he wasn't sure he knew much about prayer—that the boy would yield now, that he would not grow up to know the shameful sham that Pete's life had been.

"I love you…"

"You must not!" the boy wailed. His defense was weakening. "It isn't possible. Find someone else's identity to demolish!"

"I love…"

"You KILL!"

"I love you I love you I love you!" The Word's words were a Chinese water torture of kindness on a heart deflated by subtle abuse. That heart slowly filled as the defeated boy nursed compassion from the forest's soft floor. The beat pulsed in his veins, Life bringing life.

The boy stood to run again, the Word vibrating his very bones:

"I love you I love you I love you I love you I love I…."

And the boy's scream once more filled the forest, but now in a hauntingly different tone: "I love I love I AM loved!"

"So what happened to Pete and the boy?" I thought the story needed some kind of denouement.

"Love has a terrible impact on a false life," the old salt said. "You can be sailing blithely on a beam reach, but when love hits you its like the leading edge of a squall line off your stern. It makes a mess of your neat plans. Sometimes you have to change course completely and run with its wind. It's too strong to fight."

"OK. So what happened?" He was always teaching when I wanted answers. But I had a hunch his teaching was a warning to me.

"They lived happily ever after some of the time. The boy went back to school, became an architect, married a girl who loved his soul as he loved hers, and bought Pete's old house. Pete sold the car and the house, sank

the yacht, divorced his trophy wife, and moved to Santa Fe to make pottery. Every pot he made was filled with joy."

I wasn't sure that I understood the last piece of cargo that I was to take
back to shore. I knew this story contained it, but I couldn't quite grasp it.

My mentor gazed intently: "You ever hear religious folks talk about
being saved?"

I laughed. "Too often. I don't believe it and I don't know what it
means."

"Well," he said, "to most of them it means that God has stamped their
life with a big 'OK' like a meat inspector at a slaughterhouse so they can go
to Heaven when they die."

Heaven sounded like a pretty good deal to me. Death was inevitable, so
why not make it transitory? "If that is being saved, then I'm all for it."

"Sometimes," he yawned, "a fisherman tells a big story about a little
fish. That's what happens when people think that being saved is simply a
matter of going to Heaven."

"Isn't it?" I asked. "What's wrong with that?"

"Nothin' wrong with it. It's just too small a fish. Heaven's not in doubt
for anyone. The Spirit-force doesn't have any other place but Love's being.
No, being saved is about being changed by Love before you die."

"Like the people in the story," I thought.

"Yes. Being saved is a matter of becoming who you are, not who you
planned to be or who you thought you were. That may upset a lot of religious folks who use their beliefs as a defense against Love's storms."

"This is the last piece of cargo you want me to carry? You want me to
tell others that salvation is falling into Love's wild Spirit even if it means
that other people think you're nuts?"

"Yes." His words were serene, though their message could bring terror.

The light faded while we soaked. I knew that soon I would have to set
sail, but my heart wanted to stay with this gentle and free man. We stood
together to let the gathering breeze dry our puckered flesh. We dressed
without words and shoveled sand over the driftwood fire. My heart filled
with sadness at the thought of leaving this place and this man.

"It's time," he said. "I have given you a cargo that you must share with others. It will set many free, though most will reject it. Sail with care!"

I wept. Through my sobs I heard him say, "Watch for my dolphins!" And then he was gone. I stood alone on the sand and shells of the island I had known for years. *Moonghost* rested at anchor just offshore, her bow bobbing in growing chop. A subtropical sunset replaced the fog. I could just make out the mainland on a course of 290 degrees.

I waded to *Moonghost's* stern, lowered her swim ladder, and pulled myself aboard. I meditated for a few minutes, hauled the mainsail, set the jib, weighed anchor, trimmed the sheets, and slipped silently home.

EPILOG

▼

UNPACKING THE CARGO

My soul's voyage never ends, but I often pull into port for a long rest. During those times I don't think very much about life's purpose, God's nature, or other big questions. I simply live. I wake up in the morning beside my wife, thankful for another day to breathe. I surf the web, read a mystery, or go for a boat ride. On those days it's good just to *be*—that's the best prayer I know. My license plate frame reads, "I'd rather be boating." Some days I delete the last word.

Most cruising sailors are at sea only two or three weeks each year. The rest of the time they repair their boats, do odd jobs to replenish the kitty, then rest and enjoy the places where they have set their hooks. That's as it should be, especially on voyages of the soul. Resting is so good that God desires that we spend one-seventh of our time doing it. Voyaging is hard work: you can't scrub decks, haul sheets, and sleep at odd angles on hard surfaces all the time.

But a moment arrives when the wind fills, the tide ebbs, and Mystery calls. Then the spiritual cruiser sits at the chart table, engages the left-brain, plots a course to the next island, and enters new waypoints in the GPS. Such times come for all of us who make passages of the soul.

Resting makes us restless. There is a time for simple *being*, and there is a time for *reflecting* on being—for getting underway!

That is when we do theology. We are all theologians. Most folks in the church, or for that matter in the secular world, don't believe they do theology. That's supposed to be the job of professional scholars. But that's not how theology works. Real theology's not the esoteric rumination of scholars in ivy-covered halls. It's what you and I do whenever we think the big questions, and especially when we think the biggest questions of all: who or what is God, and what does God have to do with us, and what difference does that make about what we have to do with each other? Usually we do our theologizing in college bull sessions, in bars or AA meetings, at parties, at church when we think no one is really listening, and in conversation with spiritual friends. Rarely are we given an "Island Mystic" to scramble our assumptions and guide us to new understanding.

There's something scary happening these days on the seas of Christianism. Pirates have boarded the ship of faith and are hijacking its cargo. Most of the pirates wear red uniforms, but there some blue ones too. The crews on the pirate ships are dinosaurs—people with very small brains racing towards extinction. The red pirate chiefs tell the dinosaurs that Jesus came to create a sexually moral society where homosexuality (and maybe any kind of sexuality) and confident women are evil but greed and obsessive consumption are OK, where it's good to exploit the environment (after all, the end of the world is near so we won't need it anyway), and where the crews' insecurities are allayed by clear instructions from God about how to live. The blue pirate chiefs tell their crews that Jesus came to abolish capitalism, share truth with other religions, protect the environment, let women and gays make their own moral choices, and defend against the red pirates. Sometimes they tell their crews that there is no cargo.

"Trout Fishing in America," a brilliant popular music duo, wrote a song entitled "I Wish I Was a Dinosaur." One line describes it all: "I never think of anything I never thought before." For the pirates and their dinosaur crews there are no new thoughts, there are no new ways to resolve differences, and there is certainly no new theology. Everything that can be said about God has already been said, and each side knows their "facts" are the only truth. The dinosaurs are terrified that if they leave on a voyage of spiritual discovery they will sail off the end of the world. Of course, that might be OK since a lot of them are anxious for the end of the world anyway.

Don't be captured by the pirates! Don't become a Christianist dinosaur! Don't crowd the Spirit by loading God's ship with worn out trash and turning it into a garbage scow! Every one of us yearns to love God with our entire mind as well as with our whole heart. *Give in to the temptation to do your own theology! Think the thoughts that are yours, not the ones that have been handed down to you in creeds and traditions. Tradition is where you begin your journey, not where you end it. Write your own Bible, or at least your own version of the Bible.* Remember: when Moses found a burning bush he didn't have a reference book to tell him how to deal with it. Moses and Mystery were alone in that desert. Sooner or later it's the same for you and for me. There're just Mystery and us when we face our own burning bushes. (And we will face them often as we develop eyes to see them.) So there's a lot of freedom when it comes to understanding Mystery—freedom to voyage past the boundaries drawn by conventional religion. If you sail beyond the chart, be assured that you won't sail off the end of the world. There are no demons or sea monsters waiting to get you. God is delighted when you think new thoughts. Thinking new thoughts is one of the ways that God plays, and God smiles when we get involved in the game.

God gives me ever-greater intellectual freedom as I grow older. While my mind wonders about the "big questions," my heart grows closer to Love's presence. I spend countless hours searching log books left by others on their spiritual voyages. I listen for the Word of Love in everything I hear, and I do my best to plot my position on the spiritual seas. When sailors navigate they mark their location as an estimate, or at least they did in the days of dead reckoning and celestial navigation before GPS turned their art to science. Spiritual voyagers still use celestial navigation: we watch the heavens, listen for the Word, and make guesses about where we are. That's the best we can do. The tidal currents of the Spirit are too tricky for us to be any more precise than that. If we think we have our position firmly fixed, we've probably run aground.

In the remainder of this chapter, I share my current position on theology's charts, cruising past the landmarks of God, Jesus, religion, church, and prayer with the help of the Island Mystic's cargo. Some of my ideas are unconventional, but remember that the new reformation, the new Christianity, will be found beyond conventions. Most of these playful meditations show up in different form in the Island Mystic's parables. I hope that they will stimulate you to do your own theology. Maybe you will recognize that you have already left the land of dinosaurs and Christianism. Maybe you will discover a new Christianity flowing with currents of divine Love. And maybe you will find yourself in the company of other sailors on these new seas: their ships are named "Emerging Church" or "Narrative Theology" or "Jesus Seminar" or "Progressive Christianity," and some have no names. But all are crewed by people in love with God, fascinated with Jesus, and hopeful that a fresh wind of the Spirit is blowing. So get angry, feel doubtful, ask questions, and then dive for your own truth. It's down there. But remember: all you can bring to the surface are reflections of the light, not the Light itself. And there's no exam at Heaven's gate.

GOD

We might as well start with the big One. After all, everything begins and ends with God. (A statement neither you nor I can possibly understand.)

If everything written about God were laid end-to-end, page-by-page, it would stretch from Costa Rica to the Andromeda Galaxy. And it still wouldn't make much sense. Bible, Koran, sutras, Dharma—all try to tell who God is and isn't, and all fall short. People write biographies of God, have conversations with God, and use God as a weapon to support politics, the idol of nationalism, or superficial virtue. All also fall short.

I'm going to risk saying two things about God that I believe are true, and then, like most other people, I'll just speculate a lot. First, *God is Love: complete unconditional forgiving love*. That is the most powerful and liberating statement in the history of religion and it has yet to be appropriated completely into the thinking of religious people. God is not a little loving, God is not mildly affectionate, nor does God love most people except for gays or Jews or Muslims or feminists. No, God *is* Love. That means that it is impossible for God to be anything that is not loving. It is impossible for God to be arbitrary, capricious, exclusive, remote, vengeful, condemning, judging, or wrathful. The idea that we should fear God is bunk. Love isn't scary (although because we aren't yet transformed into Love ourselves, we may fear the way that Love that destroys our defenses, forces us to refine our self-images, and frees us from manipulating others).

It's been tough for me to give up the image of a scary god who waits in the heavens with a quiver of lightning bolts to zap me when I make a mistake. I wasn't raised with that kind of God, as are some fundamentalists, but my father was godlike in his power and when I was very young his wrath was scarier than God's. I guess I confused God and Dad a lot. Most of us do something like that. We project our fears and guilt onto God. On the voyage of our soul, we need to lighten the ship and jettison some cargo. Throw your scary god overboard! Remember: God doesn't *choose* to love. If God could choose to love, then God could also choose not to love. But if God *is* Love, then God cannot choose to be or do anything else.

The second true thing about the God of Love is that *you can't say anything else about God*, other than to explore more deeply the mystery of love. Religious leaders almost always forget this. They pontificate mightily, thereby breaking the commandment not to use God's name in vain. Most talk about God is vain, empty, and just plain wrong. Often it's best simply to be quiet. Those closest to God are like Trappist monks: their spiritual growth is measured by the quality of their silence.

Like most Christians, I managed to grow up in the church without any exposure to our mystical tradition. Throughout study for two graduate theological degrees I was taught nothing about Bernard, Patrick, Hildegard, Eckhart, Julian, Teresa of Avila, Porete, or Merton. I remember one conversation about mysticism with a fellow Christian. When I spoke of mystical Christianity, she responded, "It isn't possible to use 'mystic' and 'Christian' in the same sentence." Most Christians would say the same thing. Our mystics have been slandered by (masculinist linear-thinking) church historians. Most Christians, if they have heard of mystics at all, think they were weird, theologically unorthodox, and irrelevant. Our mystics have been ignored, imprisoned, or executed by ecclesiastical powers. But they experienced union with God, and their hearts exploded with poetry and praise of the One who was their friend. Their God could be known by Love's heart but not defined by the mind. Love, after all, is Mystery.

The mystics of our tradition knew a passion for God that transcends words. When they spoke of God at all it was usually as *via negativa*: that is, if you want to describe God, you can only say what God is *not*. With the exception of saying that God is Love, I agree with them. Knowing that we can't describe God gives us great freedom. It's fun to start thinking of all the things that God isn't.

Now let's join God in some playful speculation. We've already said that God isn't negative, condemning, judgmental, exclusive, remote, wrathful, vengeful, scary, or capricious. Here are some more things that God isn't:

- *God is not the Supreme Being.* In fact, God isn't *a* "being" at all, in the sense that you, frogs, parrots, or paramecia are beings. It is impossible, here or "in" heaven, to point in one direction and say "There's God," and to point in another direction and say "God isn't over there." For reasons I'll discuss a little later, in our new quantum understanding of reality God is too pervasive and vast to be a discrete and separate being. It might be better to think this way: God is who or what makes beings possible. Without God there wouldn't be any locusts or jellyfish. That's why some people, like Meister Eckhart and the great theologian Paul Tillich, spoke of God as the "ground" of being rather than "a" being.

- *God is not the universe.* A lot of New Age people, who are trying to avoid using the word "God" in vain, as religious people often do, have started talking about the universe as though it were God. The universe is incomprehensively huge, but it isn't God. The world of quantum physics tells us that there may be an infinite number of universes, all existing at the same time. To personalize our universe and speak of it as a being with divine power is to use a metaphor of God that is too limited. God is what makes the infinite number of parallel universes possible.

- *God is not a king, nor is God a queen.* The metaphor of a monarch was a good one to use in the ancient world, and Jesus got a lot of mileage out of it, but it has seen its better days. No one today knows what a king really is. There are a lot of figurehead monarchs in our world, but none who fully embody the archetype of a ruler. (Of course, for a lot of people God *is* a king because God is just a figurehead as well.) The world is growing up and so is our consciousness. We need a God who relates to us more as guide and friend than as potentate and top dog in the hierarchy. Monarchs are remote and unapproachable. Love is present and intimate. Anyway, if God is not *a* being among other beings, then it makes no sense to say God is *a* monarch. As a matter of fact, it makes no sense to say that God is any-*thing*.

- *God is not a Christian. God is not a Muslim, a Hindu, a Buddhist, a Jew, or an aboriginal shaman.* I have said this before, but it cannot be said too often. When any of us forget this great truth and claim God as our own, we then feel justified in killing, physically or spiritually, anyone who disagrees with us. We feel a great need to defend our God and to prove others wrong. We are actually only defending our ego's need to control life's outrageous slings and arrows, and we easily deny the motives for our actions when we decide that God is on our side. Beware of anyone who belongs to the "one true" religion, for sooner or later that person will find an excuse to persecute you in God's name.

- This list could continue *ad nauseum*. We've already said that God does not judge, condemn, turn away from us, punish, get really angry and destroy the world, cause cancer or AIDS, or start wars to depose bad rulers.

When speculation about God reaches this point, then it's fun to think of new images that might be useful since the old images and metaphors are worn out. After all, God warned us not to make graven images. The most dangerous images are those that we engrave on our minds. I think that

God is a lot happier when we are a little playful about her/him. Lest you believe that I am being disrespectful of God in the paragraphs that follow, remember the multiplicity of images that biblical writers used: God as a writer, a king, a judge, a mother, a father, a daddy, a hen, an archer, a stream, a spirit, a landowner, a widow, and so on. People talk about God in the language of their worldview and experience. Because of our changing understanding of science and the human psyche, we need to update our own God-language.

Our era is on the brink of a completely new way of understanding the physical world. As our models of reality change, our metaphors of God must change with them. We are learning that our perception of the material world is more a matter of social agreement than a reflection of reality. Even the Earth may be more like a hot air balloon than a solid rock. At the heart of every atom is a plethora of energy systems that sometimes appear to be particles but often act like waves moving through vast empty space. Quarks love each other, and neutrinos are lonely and shy. For those of us who still look at life through the lens of Newton's familiar physics, this quantum view of reality puts us in the same class as those who thought the world was flat in 1492. Physical reality may not exist at all. When we consider the theories of subatomic physics, new notions about God seem rather simple by comparison. In a quantum universe, which can only be understood using the mental gymnastics of imaginary numbers and in which all matter is energy that has slowed down its intensity of vibration, there is plenty of room to play with new and fun metaphors about God. Here are a few of my favorites:

- *God is like invisible plasma* that fills every space of this and all universes. This is a long way from saying that God is a king on a throne in heaven. Plasma is a difficult concept to describe briefly. Imagine it as the fourth state of matter, after solids, liquids, and gases. It consists of electrons and ions that move freely throughout the universe. Even though it can't be seen, touched, or smelled, NASA has used it to power a space probe and generate electricity for the space station. It provides a useful metaphor for God: a powerful reality that is in and through everything yet beyond our limited senses. Still, this seems a little rarified. It's difficult to build a loving relationship with plasma. No one is likely to pray, "Our Plasma whose heavenly ions fill the universe...."

- *God is like a field.* This image will sound a lot like the last one, but I like it better. I don't mean that God is a place where you can plant corn. I mean that God is like a magnetic field. Fields surround us and are even inside us, but we can't experience them in normal ways. They influence our lives without our knowledge. Some people now say that magnetic fields can help heal us. I don't know about that, but I do know that language about fields sounds a lot like language about God. Suppose that God is a field, similar to an electromagnetic field, and that this and all universes are inside of that field. Maybe Jesus was like a new physicist when he said, "The kingdom of heaven is like a treasure hidden in a field...."

- *God is like big invisible goo.* My stepdaughter Caitlin plays with some stuff that is slimy, transparent, and shapeless. It came in a plastic container with some "solid" things floating in it. When I touched the solid things, they were gooey like the medium they floated in, just more viscous. God and we are like that. God is the goo in which we live and move and have our being. We're made out of God-stuff, just a little denser than God. I think that this image is fun but I can't imagine the psalmist singing, "Who are humans that you are mindful of us, yet you have made us a little more viscous than the angels?"

- *God is the wind in our sails.* I like this one. We have to adjust our lives to move with the wind of God. No sailor controls the breeze, though the mariner may try to "whistle it up" or pray for it to abate. The best we can do in our tiny boats is to pay attention to its direction and trim our craft in harmony with it. Our life with God is like that.

- *God is mind, and we are archetypes.* This one can be a little more confusing than the others. If quantum physics changes the way we think about nature, Carl Jung's depth psychology changes the way we think about soul and our deep psyche. Jung was a student of Freud who parted ways with him over the reality of the spiritual life. Freud thought that spiritual life and religion were ways to assuage Oedipal guilt and rage. Sexual energy powered the personality and was indiscriminate in its longings. In contrast, Jung asserted that spirituality, not sexuality, drives the personality. The "archetype" is one of Jung's more difficult concepts. It's something like this: inside our psyches exist some "parts" that are almost like autonomous beings. Their stories are told in myth, art, poetry, and scripture, such as the stories of the Greek gods. We talk about them as though they were separate spiritual beings, but, actually, they are part of us. Mars, Venus, Mercury, Zeus, and the complete Greek and Roman pantheon are archetypes within our minds. We have a three-ring circus of semi-autonomous critters all wanting to be center-stage inside our heads. Now, in the same way, we can apply this to ourselves and God. God's mind is the only mind there is. You, your favorite enemy, your worst lover, and I are all semi-autonomous parts of the mind of God. We act and think as though we are independent of God, but that's a delusion of the ego's consciousness. Thinking that we are separate from God is spiritual insanity. The truth is that we don't find our real identity until we lose the one we think we have. Then, in our emptiness, we discover fullness in God. That's what Jesus meant when he said we had to lose ourselves to find ourselves.

All of these images are similar. Maybe I was a better theologian when I was four years old. One dark and stormy night in our old brick house I snuggled deep into my blankets and shivered at the thunder's boom. A frog-strangling rain beat on the awning above my open window, and I was scared. My mother reassured me that God watched over me. I looked out the window but didn't see God anywhere. I asked where God was hiding. She laughed and said that God is everywhere and that God doesn't hide. I've been thinking about that night ever since.

Each of these images says that God is everywhere, and that God doesn't hide. In fact, there is no way to escape God—not because God is in us, but because we are in God. My favorite way to think of God these days is like a "Spirit force." I don't know what Spirit is. I can't define it. But like electrically charged plasma, it empowers me. Like a field, it affects me. Like goo, I am immersed in it and made from its substance. Like wind, it moves me when I attune myself to it. And like mind, it is thought beyond my own thought. Spirit's a little like the old Supreme Court judge's definition of pornography: "I don't know how to define it, but I know it when I see it." Spirit-force flows from beyond this and all universes, permeating all that is, seen and unseen, with its nature. It influences every choice we make. It influences the unfolding of all evolution. And it leads everything toward Love.

We live in this Spirit like a fish lives in water. It affects us like ocean currents affect that fish, sometimes moving us so subtly that we don't know it is happening. This force is inevitably personal because it is the essence and source of Love, and so we experience it as "a" person with discrete boundaries and being.

So have fun thinking of your own images of God. Remember "The Master's Lunch:" you can make any kind of peanut butter sandwich you want, but be sure to include the peanut butter. You can make lots of images of God, but be sure that they all are built around Love. Read scriptures, learn from others' experiences, and then follow your own heart and imagination. God will enjoy you while you do it, and you will enjoy God.

JESUS

Some sailors never race. Even before the America's Cup was lost to the Kiwis, those sailors knew they couldn't compete with Dennis Connor. And some golfers left the PGA. They knew that no one could defeat Tiger Woods. Why jump on the dog pile if you can't be the top dog in a competitive world?

We've turned Jesus into the Dennis Connor or Tiger Woods of the spiritual life. We've made him so superhuman that he is often a source of discouragement and futility rather than a source of inspiration. No one measures up to the "only Son of God." Parents, pastors, and teachers tell us to be like him. Entrepreneurs market bracelets and T-shirts emblazoned with WWJD, as though a generation of young people could become transcendental mind readers. They profit from the illusion that Jesus' decisions and actions are so easily stereotyped that anyone with a minimum of biblical knowledge can make difficult ethical decisions by asking what Jesus would do. The "imitation of Christ" has become an unachievable guideline for life that produces a sense of failure in disciples. It is cruel to impose a standard on persons that no one can achieve.

Not even Jesus measures up to what we have done to him since his death and resurrection. Sometimes when I read the gospels I find Jesus saying things that I don't believe he would have said. I now think that these "unJesuslike" sayings were edited into the text generations after Jesus was here. Surely Jesus didn't think of himself as God in a human suit. He didn't step into a phone booth and emerge as a spiritual superman when someone needed to be healed or the Pharisees were out of line. But there remains something amazingly captivating about him. Something about Jesus grips us in ways that Buddha and other spiritual masters do not.

Beneath the labels (Messiah, Christ, Son of God, Son of Man, Rabbi, Master, Lord) is a *person* whose presence we know. I have no clue how this happens! I don't think that anyone explains it very well. I know that his nature must be exactly like my own or his life would have no relevance to mine. I also know that he lived his life with openness to Spirit-force and Love in ways that I do not. That is the difference between us. That is what the labels try to explain. It's as though Jesus is like you or me, only more so.

I don't do academic Christology. I'll leave that to theology professors. But we all do a little informal Christology when we bump up against the uniqueness of Jesus. Here's my latest: *Jesus was totally permeable to the presence of Spirit-force.* All of us are open to it some of the time, but he was open to it all of the time. *He is what/who we are at heart.*

We live in a strange era. We know our genome, we dig into our psychology, we use drugs to control our neurochemistry, but we don't know much about being human. We stockpile nuclear and biological weapons, we ignore genocide and poverty in the third world, we allow diseases to run rampant that could be easily cured, and we let people die of starvation that we could easily feed. Despite all we know about humanity, we still haven't figured out how to be human.

We need Jesus more than ever if we are to survive as a species. Jesus shows our full potential and our true nature. To the extent that he was a

Jewish reformer and messiah, he was limited by history and culture just as we are today. We continue to try to contain him within the boundaries of Christianism's dogmas. But Jesus is bigger than our traditions. To the extent that his life and message are transparent to Spirit and reflect Spirit's compassion, he is a bearer of universal light and can be found within every spiritual tradition. I see Jesus in Buddha, in Socrates, in Chief Seattle, in the Dalai Lama, in Thich Nhat Hanh, and in Nelson Mandela. Sometimes I see Jesus in myself, in my wife and children, and in the checkout clerk at the supermarket. Just as there is only one Mind, there is only one human Person. Jesus shows us that we are fully human when we discover that our true nature is Love. Love is our only hope. It is who we are.

RELIGION

Religion's gone crazy these days. Clergy foment division and conflict rather than peace, love, and reconciliation. Politicians tell us that they are on God's side but act like God is on their side. Terrorists kill civilians for God, and governments kill terrorists for God. It's time to bring some sanity to religion.

I remember a stormy winter day in Rockport, Texas. A blue norther tore up the Gulf while I sat by the fire with an old copy of Joshua Slocum's classic *Sailing Alone Around the World.* There's a lot to be learned as an armchair sailor. I can share the ecstasy of a starlit night watch or marvel at the flying fish before my bow on a downwind run. I can learn to survive in thirty-foot seas and what to do when my rudder breaks. I can find the etiquette for a *kava* ceremony in the South Pacific or where to snorkel in the Virgin Islands. But my experience is second-hand until I actually cast off the moorings and go to sea. Memorizing Jimmy Buffett's songs doesn't make me a blue-water cruiser any more than memorizing scripture verses makes me a person of love.

As a sailor of the soul, I revel in Thomas Merton's struggle to be an authentic contemplative within the boundaries of monastic life. I quiet my mind with the meditations of Thich Nhat Hanh. I enjoy Walsch's conversations with God which mirror my own prayerful dialog with the Spirit-force of Love. I wonder what it took for Abraham to leave home at such an old age and why Moses was willing to leave Midian to return to Egypt. I am moved by the courage of Nathan and Jeremiah and Amos and the occasional tenderness of Isaiah. I am encouraged by the Buddha's persistent search for answers to the riddles of human suffering. I am touched by Julian's sweet wisdom and thrilled by Hildegard's sense of wonder. I learn from all these and more as I did from the blue-water cruisers. These are some of the great soul sailors who have been powered by the winds of Spirit. I may be religious but I will never be spiritual until I actually open my heart to Spirit as they did. Religion without heart quickly becomes demonic and destructive.

Religion is a vessel for truth, not truth itself. *Religion is second-hand mysticism.* Mystics encounter God directly. Others are drawn to them by the aura of God, follow them, and write of their experiences. Those writings touch the hearts of still others and become scripture. And those scriptures become codified prescriptions for the behavior of all. Then religions are born and our wild God is brought under control. The free force of Spirit is tamed. Maps are drawn, and the map-keepers allow no new explorations.

Religion is one of the most powerful of all social energies. Because it is *almost* truth and truth itself cannot be defined, lazy and anxious but heart-hungry followers make a deal with tradition: "I'll give up searching for my own experience of God if you will make me feel secure, give me a way to cope with death, and find some people who will accept me." Once this deal is cut, the follower has a corner on truth, and others who believe differently are cast out or even killed. More people are slaughtered in the name of religion than in any other cause. The world is full of bad religion. But, thankfully, good religion happens.

Good religion has two marks: it is *tentative* and it is *transparent*. It holds its beliefs tightly but lightly, compassionately aware that others hold their beliefs with similar tenacity. It knows that it could be wrong about some things and that others may be right about some things. Good religion does not draw attention to itself but to its hope that others see God through its practice. When religious people forget these two marks, they create a fortress of fear where they hide from the wild mystery of God and threaten anyone who approaches the fortress walls.

I often tell this Zen story when I preach. An old master stood before his disciples, lifted his arm, extended his finger, and pointed toward the full moon. "It is beautiful," he exclaimed. A few disciples murmured with joyful insight while others built a monument to the master's finger. In ages that followed, devotees knelt before paintings of that extended finger, placed replicas of it on altars, and carried it on key-chains in their pockets and purses.

True religion is a pointer, not a container. If it contains anything it all, it never puts a lid on it. Wisely, every generation or so, someone shatters the container and lets truth find fresh expression. "We have this treasure," Paul said, "in earthen vessels." That's religious sanity.

CHURCHES

Churches mirror their religions. They are inevitable. They are capable of great good. But they tend toward subtle evil. I've had a love-hate relationship with churches all of my life. Generally I find them oppressive. Sometimes I can scarcely breathe during worship services. I want to run out of the building screaming and warning others to stay away. Yet at other times I am deeply moved, and in rare moments I find individuals who have transcended the boundaries of their church to inspire me with their Love. Those persons are a puzzle to me. I don't understand how an institution that is so bound by tradition and fear can contain a few persons who love with freedom and courage.

We humans gather with like-minded people. That's why churches are inevitable. We are incurably communal. Even the desert hermits of the fourth century met from time to time to discuss how best to live alone. Real churches have the same marks as real religion. They are *tentative* and they are *transparent*. They don't put down others who practice faith differently, and others see God in their common life. Real churches are hard to find.

But religious clubs are on every block. Sometimes there are several of them in the same block. They compete for members in the religious market, run ads in the paper bearing pictures of smiling pastors with sculpted hair, build bowling alleys and gyms for Jesus, and erect giant billboards that portray the glories of their leaders but don't say anything about God. Religious clubs are not transparent. It would be difficult for an anthropologist to distinguish them from any other business. In their teaching they appeal to the left hemisphere of the brain and to the defenses of the ego: "God only loves those who are right. We are right. God loves us, but we're not sure of other people." There's neither mystery nor inclusion in a religious club.

But we have to begin our spiritual journeys somewhere. Before I learned to sail from a master, I went to a sailing school for beginners. Only later, when I had some feel for helm and hull, did I learn the finer arts, and only later still did I attempt to single-hand my vessel. Religious clubs are like large-scale sailing schools. They are good places to get introduced to the spiritual life, but they don't take you on the journey. People who never graduate from sailing school get landlocked after awhile. That's the way it is with lots of churches. They're full of people who quit growing a long time ago and settled for second-hand faith. No wonder they're scared of change. They sold adventure with God for a slice of security or, worse, duty.

Our contemporary religious landscape has some intriguing inconsistencies. The new religious clubs, usually very strict, very literal in their use of scripture, and very savvy in media and advertising are growing like hurricanes in September. The old religious clubs, the ones we once called "mainline" churches, are declining like the relics they have become: old ships in dry-dock, rotting and barnacle-encrusted hulls where members gather for sea-stories but stay away from any body of water larger than a puddle in the parking lot. The shipwrecked mainline churches have failed in their mission. They expend energy arguing about who's in and who's out (this year it's gays, but last year it was women, and before that it was blacks) instead of providing a "next-step" for those whose spiritual growth leads them beyond the introductory religious clubs. A lot of growing Christians have nowhere to go. They often give up their faith, thinking that it has nothing more to offer them. Others hang on, feed on the few crumbs that the dying mainline gives them and hope that someday they, too, can find a community of like-minded people. But more and more Christians simply live in exile from Christianism.

For decades America's Cup racers designed Twelve Meter boats. They didn't all look alike, but they weren't very different either, a lot like churches of today. Then New Zealand did the unthinkable and took the Cup south. Now America's Cup designs change before every series. The breakdown of an old system made a new period of creativity possible. Today's spiritual communities are like that. The old styles worked for a long time but they don't work very well anymore. New vessels are emerging. Some are just new facades for the old time clubs. Some are fresh from God's drawing board.

It's time for something completely different—no point in looking for the Holy Grail where you already know it isn't. The "church" of the 21st century may have no buildings. It may have no membership lists. It will have fewer religious professionals and less need for them. It may look more like a network than an organization. Groups will form, meet as long as their needs and purpose require, and then disband without censure. They will not spend money or energy on their own survival. They will never sponsor the "Fiftieth Annual First Church Bazaar" or solicit money from communities they should be serving. Their purpose will be to open the hearts of those who share their life. They will always be tentative and they will always be transparent to God: a spiritual community of loving hearts, formed by the movement of the Spirit, and by nature open, receptive, inclusive, accepting, and without judgment.

PRAYER

This is a tough one. It should be easy. Sooner or later everybody prays. The old saying, "There are no atheists in foxholes," fits the sailor. When a severe squall sweeps across the water towards a (suddenly very small) boat, there are four things the captain always does: plot the present position, shorten sail, check the ground tackle or sea anchor for possible use, and pray.

I disliked most prayer when I was a kid. The minister's pastoral prayers were long, boring, and flowery. I fidgeted, felt ashamed for feeling resentful, and wanted to run out of the sanctuary. The physical attitude of prayer—bowed head, silence, listening to someone talk for too long—felt like punishment. It was the same position I assumed when my father was lecturing me. During that same time my mother taught me a bedtime prayer: "Now I lay me down to sleep…. If I should die…." There wasn't much comfort in a prayer that reminded me that I might die that night. I often was too scared to fall asleep. At least she taught the habit of praying as part of my bedtime ritual.

I was liberated from the shame of prayer when I discovered liturgy in the Episcopal and Catholic churches. The prayers continued even when I didn't have anything to say. The books covered all the bases and freed me from the obligation to think profound thoughts in order to get God's attention on a busy Sunday morning. But even though I had the *Book of Common Prayer* to carry me, something was still wrong in my inner life. I heard others talk of praying for hours, and I didn't know what they meant. Pastors taught that prayer was the foundation of a life of faith. I didn't get it. I wanted to, but I couldn't find the key.

Being told that you must pray but never being taught how to do it is a little like being thrown overboard and hoping you will learn to swim when you hit the water. For most of my adult life and all of my childhood, I thought that prayer was a matter of asking for help or apologizing for failure. That's the kind of prayer that soldiers and sailors offer in moments of crisis. I usually felt diminished by such prayer and wondered why a God of Love wouldn't act until I pleaded with him to do something. I don't think I'm alone in this reaction to prayer. The very word is rooted in the concept of begging a king for a favor. Legal language still uses it that way today. In the courts lawyers "pray" to judges for favors. Begging a king for a favor implies the possibility that he might refuse it, regardless of its worth. A capricious monarch (or god) doesn't offer unconditional Love. It's hard to trust a God whose desire depends upon my use of the proper words.

In 1971 I attended a young pastors' retreat at a Catholic convent that was in the throes of post-Vatican II reform. The sisters stocked their bookstore with all manner of new ideas and I left a fair amount of my money there. While other young pastors played tennis, drank beer, went to topless clubs, and otherwise rebelled against the strictures of their roles, I sat in my small cell reading Thomas Merton's *Contemplative Prayer.* I was never the same afterwards. I discovered that all of life is prayer. I had been praying as a child when I spent hours lying on the grass looking at clouds. I had been praying when I read Plato or Kant, when I rode my horse across a windy ridge, and when I listened to Beethoven or Copland or Hank Williams. I had been praying when I talked and listened with friends as we shared our inner lives.

Prayer became easy when I learned that it is simply a matter of falling into Love. In the embrace of a divine Lover and Friend, I do not feel like a lesser subject asking favors of a fearsome monarch. The one who loves me will never demean me or refuse his/her presence. If I ask a favor or utter a desperate plea, I am not begging from a power that would refuse me. Every prayer for Love's presence is answered.

Merton set me on a new path. Along the way I had some charismatic experience, though I was wary of the distortions of the movement that went with it, and I learned joy and ecstasy in the assurance that God is not "out there" somewhere but deep within my own heart. I became a "truth diver." I no longer view prayer as a matter of asking or begging. Prayer is a way of relating, often without words in the wondrous solitude of silence. Because of prayer and the one I meet in others, in nature, and in my heart I have been forced to rethink my whole view of God, religion, the spiritual life, and the church.

Prayer is dangerous. It leads us outside the boundaries of secondhand mysticism. It sets us free to think our own thoughts. We sit beside God rather than kneeling before a throne. We share life with a God who is our friend and constant companion, not a distant parent or monarch. And we discover that every bush burns if the eyes of our heart can see the flames.

Prayer turns all of us into island mystics.

It's time to rest in port for a while. I could continue these reflections but that would be too much cargo for one shipment. I have come to view theology as the mind's playful prayer, born of a trusting heart's overflow. I have enjoyed playing with you in these pages.

Do not accept everything in these parables as truth, but don't be afraid to admit that some of them carry God's Word within them. Do your own truth diving! The cargo I carried back to port on *Moonghost* helped me on my own voyage of the soul. The Island Mystic that fed me breakfast and filled my empty hold will stay with me the rest of my life. I hope he has helped you as well. It is difficult to be a follower of Jesus in the era of Christianism's death. Perhaps he has given you the courage to sail beyond tradition's boundaries, the freedom to shed ideas that have constricted your spirit, and the wisdom to plot your own soul's course. You do not voyage alone.

These conversations must end for now, but more cargo awaits us on another island. Until our next voyage, pay attention to the rhumb line of Love as you tack through life's fog. Look deeply into life for the living Word's Presence. Let prayer be your GPS and your heart will receive guidance from above. And keep a watch for those emerald dolphins.

The End

978-0-595-40028-7
0-595-40028-0

Printed in the United States
64459LVS00005B/106-153

9 780595 400287